# CHORUS OF WHISPERS

# CHORUS OF WHISPERS

SARAH HANS

Dragon's Roost Press

Printed in the United States of America

Ingram ISBN: 978-1-956824-38-4

Print ISBN 978-1-956824-30-8

Digital ISBN 978-1-956824-31-5

Dragon's Roost Press

2470 Hunter Rd.

Brighton, MI 48114

thedragonsroost.biz

# DEDICATION

*For Paisley*

# CONTENTS

# INTRODUCTION

## LUCY A. SNYDER

Dear Reader,

Welcome to *Chorus of Whispers* by Sarah Hans! I congratulate you on your excellent taste or extremely good fortune, depending on whether you've specifically sought out this book or just happened to open it while you were browsing someone's stack (or an online storefront) at random. Either way, I envy you, because you get to read these stories for the very first time!

I've known Sarah as a fellow writer for a very long time. Long enough that my brain is certain that she has always lived in the castle of the Columbus writing community, even though logically I know that can't be true. At this point, we've shared Tables of Contents in a whole lot of anthologies: *Bless Your Mechanical Heart, Novus Monstrum, Stitched Lips, On Wings of Steam*, and *Never Too Old to Save the World* are just a few, and all were original homes to some of the tales in this collection.

As you might guess from the titles of those anthologies, Sarah writes across a wide range of genres. She's got the goods when it comes to speculative fiction: whether you're looking for unsettling suburban gothic creepery, post-apocalyptic adventure, edges-of-ideas science fiction, dystopian alternate history, dark fairy tales, or Lovecraftian sword and sorcery, she has something you'll enjoy. (If you're looking for smut, you will not find that in this collection, but Sarah probably won't mind if I suggest the work of Winter Blair, a mutual friend of ours.)

As a writer, Sarah works with themes that are near and dear to my own dark little heart, particularly body horror. The human body is an amazing organic machine, but it's also weird and gross and full of stinky fluids. So many fluids, and so few are easy to get out of your carpet. In the vein of fluids and stains, Sarah's work also deals with the horrors and fears surrounding pregnancy and parenthood. Which, given the steady erosion of reproductive rights in this country, is extremely (and unfortunately) topical.

Sarah, not one to pull any punches, alerts you to this ongoing theme right away in her opening story, "Tiny Teeth." That one's a banger, folks. (And here I feel compelled to point out that its thematic similarities with Gretchen Felker-Martin's brilliant *Manhunt* are a case of convergent evolution. *Pseudopod* released "Teeth" well before *Manhunt* was available for advance reading.) "Tiny Teeth," "Madre," and "Dylan" form a cross-genre triptych about the perils of parenthood.

Another theme that Sarah works with is that of a woman or girl with powers that are not respected in the world (or by the family) she was born into. The power could be something supernatural, but it could be a more mundane ability like intelligence. You'll find this theme used to great effect in the title story, "Chorus of Whispers," but it's also integral to "The Last Monster of the Nine Realms," "A Legacy of Ghosts," "The Moon In Her Eyes," and "Take the Fire From Her." As a woman who grew up being told to make myself smaller to fit in, to diminish myself lest people find me to be "too much" or "too intense" ... I can personally relate a whole lot to a girl who just can't stop burning things down.

Another thing I appreciate about Sarah's fiction is her approach to endings. I think this is where her career as an educator leaks into her work as a writer the most. Her stories are accessible, easy to get into, immersive once you're inside them ... but she does not spoon-feed you a conclusion. In some cases, the full consequences of the story are left to the readers' imaginations, or to their ability to piece together subtext from earlier in the narrative. And in other cases, the end of the story is clearly the beginning of an even grander tale that might inspire daydreams or nightmares.

And, as a reader, I really enjoy that. Stories in which everything is tied up and presented to you with a neat bow on the end ... well, frankly, those bore me a little. I like stories that force me to think, tales that fire up my own imagination, narratives that present me with a bit of a puzzle that my brain will work on long after I've finished reading.

But that's enough from me. It's time for you to start reading this collection. Enjoy the dark worlds that Sarah Hans has created for your imaginative pleasures.

Lucy A. Snyder
Columbus OH
June 7, 2024

# TINY TEETH

I risk walking to the doctor's office from my workplace, because it's only a few blocks, and I think the fresh air will do me some good. I don't tell anyone I'm going alone, or that I'm walking. I know what they'll say. Outside without an escort, without the safety of an enclosed vehicle, my heart thrums like a tap dancer's quick steps. I should be scared or thrilled by the prospect of imminent danger, but I'm too frightened of the news waiting for me at the doctor's office to be worried about much else. As I walk, I become more and more convinced the news reports about the gangs of feral children, with their pictures of mutilated bodies and wide-eyed reporters speaking in quavering voices, are attempts to manipulate us with fear. To keep us inside. My coworkers are fools to walk in groups, to rush from their cars to the office with Tasers and pistols clutched in their fists. There is no danger here.

But then I see the girl, and I know I've made a mistake. She crouches behind a bush, and when I spot her, I freeze like a rabbit. She locks eyes with me and rises out of the greenery. She's maybe four years old, though that's a guess. It can be hard to tell the age of a child who has been feral a long time, and I've never been around many children to begin with, even before the virus made them violent.

She wears a tiny pair of denim shorts and a purple t-shirt decorated with glitter hearts, both caked with gore. Her hair was once styled in pigtails, but one side droops sadly, and the other side is a crusted mass of red-brown scab in place of hair. Her face is twisted into a permanent snarl. Her front two teeth are missing, which would make the expression she wears comical if she didn't have her hands held at the ready, fingers extended to grab, filthy fingernails ready to claw. A growl issues from low in her throat. Her eyes—bright green, shimmering like beetle wings in the sunlight—are filled with hatred and bloodlust. She smells like stale urine and blood and roadkill.

I fumble the pepper spray from my pocket as she lurches toward me. I hold down the trigger and close my eyes, flinching away from the stream. I remember the instructions: always aim, always look where you're pointing your weapon. But I can't look. I make a sound, a sort of squeal, the sound of a trapped herbivore facing a predator.

When I open my eyes, the girl is gone. Eyes squinted tightly shut and breath held against the burning cloud of pepper spray, I run the rest of the way to the doctor's office.

Dr. Heiss steeples his hands on the desk. Behind him, the nurse flashes me a tight, sympathetic smile. I know what he's going to say before he says it.

"Congratulations, Hailey. You're going to be a mother." He delivers the news as if it's a pizza: factually, without inflection, without excitement or dread. But at least he has the good sense not to smile.

The tight knot in my stomach unfurls and bile rises in my throat. The nurse, who isn't much older than I am, brings me water in a paper cup. I gulp it down, my swallows very loud in the quiet room. "How do I get an abortion?"

The nurse stiffens and moves away from me. Dr. Heiss frowns. "Legally, in this state, I'm not allowed to discuss the option. We can make an appointment for you with the gynecologist next door. You'll like her a lot. She can guide you through the pregnancy."

My heart hammers and the edges of my vision become ragged. I think of the girl with one pigtail, her depraved expression flashing in my mind, and a shudder ripples through me. "That's it? You're handing me a death sentence, just like that?"

He exchanges a look with the nurse, sighs, and leans back in his chair, letting his hands go to the armrests. "It's not a death sentence."

I crush the paper cup in my fist and throw it at him as I rise. "Fifty percent chance, Dr. Heiss. Fifty percent chance. I've been your patient for ten years and that's the best you can offer me?"

"I'm sorry," he sighs, "but you knew the risks."

I pace the waiting room and bite my nails down to ragged nubs. I feel like I'm going to crawl out of my own skin, so I have to move. I don't want to risk going outside alone, not with the girl maybe out there, but the waiting room feels like a jail cell.

There's a woman sitting there with her kid on a leash and I can't stop staring at them both. The woman is gaunt, hollow-eyed, and her son—it's hard to tell a kid's gender through the muzzle, but the t-shirt with a cartoon backhoe is probably a good indication he's a boy—sits on the floor trying to rip off the oven mitts taped over his hands. Going by his height, he's maybe three years old. He growls every time someone enters the office, and every time I pace past him. Everyone else in the waiting room sits on the far side, as far away from him as they can get, staring at their phones, pretending he isn't the most grotesquely fascinating thing in the room.

My phone dings when I receive the text from Tyler: *I'm here.* I move for the door and the boy snarls and lunges at me, spittle flying. He brushes me with an oven mitt before his mother yanks his leash. I step out the door into the fresh air.

I slide into the passenger seat of Tyler's sedan. "What's going on, Hail?" His eyes are intense, frantic. He's guessed why I went to the doctor.

"I'm pregnant."

"We used protection."

"Urine tests don't lie."

"Did you sleep with anyone else?" His voice takes on an edge of panic.

I'm too numb to even be upset he's asking me that. "No, of course not."

"I just don't understand how this could happen."

"No birth control is one hundred percent safe," I hear myself saying, echoing Dr. Heiss. "Abstinence is the only way to be sure."

"Okay, so, how do we get rid of it?"

Seagulls wheel and shriek over the parking lot, looking for dropped tidbits. A couple approach the door to the doctor's office and the gulls flap away. The man is pushing a stroller. The toddler strapped inside, wearing a pink dress and a muzzle decorated with shiny plastic jewels, screams like a banshee. The sound makes it impossible to think. Her open mouth is pink and red and her teeth are like white needles, snapping at the air. Her father walks robotically to the door, but her mother, for just an instant, meets my gaze through the windshield. In her eyes I see regret and exhaustion and bone-deep sorrow. She turns and goes into the office and the door shuts behind them, thankfully cutting off the screams.

"Can we just go home?" I ask.

"Can you give me a second to process this?" Tyler answers.

I sigh. "Abortions are illegal now." Nobody would have children anymore if they weren't.

"There has to be a way." His hands grip the steering wheel hard, as if he's imagining strangling his problems away.

"Of course there's a way. But I can't exactly google it." My pregnancy is on record now. If something happens to the fetus, I have to be able to document a miscarriage, or I'll face jail time. It's pretty much my worst nightmare. I want to scream at Tyler that this is his fault, because I want someone to blame, and if we sit here much longer, I'm going to do it. Tears sting my eyes. "Can we please go home? We have some time to figure this out."

"How long do we have?"

I press one hand against my abdomen. It doesn't feel any different yet. How is it possible there's a tiny monster in there, waiting to rip its way out of me? It doesn't seem real. "Dr. Heiss said they can't test for the virus until the second trimester. I'm about a month along. So we have about two months to figure it out. Obviously I want this thing out of me sooner rather than later, but it doesn't have to be right this second." I do want it out right this second, but I need time to calm down, think, strategize. I can't just tell him to drive to the grocery store and and buy me a gallon of bleach to drink.

But damn, I want to.

~

My friend Anna knows a woman. For a fee, she'll make a concoction. "It's one hundred percent safe," Anna tells me. "Legally speaking, anyway. It's all natural, too."

"What'll it do to me?"

She shrugs. "Nothing that fetus isn't going to do to you if you let it get any bigger."

Anna goes with me. I want Tyler to see this through with me, but I know better than to ask him. He already won't look at me, his eyes sliding away from mine as if repelled by a magnet.

I'm losing him. I need this thing out of me and over with as quickly as possible so we can get back to our lives.

The woman's house is on Fourth Street, in the dangerous part of town, a place I don't often go. I glance anxiously at each shadow, jumping every time a bush rustles, but I take comfort from Anna's confidence. She saunters up to the front door like she's done this a lot, which she probably has. She's always been the risk-taker in our friendship. I'm the boring one who stays at home and watches movies in my pajamas while Anna's out clubbing. Not for the first time, I'm thankful for her resourcefulness, her bravery, and the path she's blazed ahead of me. The gratitude almost chokes out the fear.

Almost. Down the street, under a streetlamp, there's a silhouette of a small person, a small person with one pigtail and her hands held up, ready to rip and tear. She's too far away for me to hear her, but I can almost feel the thrumming of her growl in my bones.

When the woman answers the door, Anna has to speak, because I'm temporarily paralyzed. "Hey, Dee."

Dee is short, shorter even than I am, with white hair and a nose too big for her face. She narrows her rheumy eyes at us but nods understanding and opens the door, beckoning us in with a casual gesture. I glance back at the streetlamp, and when I'm sure the silhouette is no longer there, I follow Anna into the house. It smells like herbs—every herb except weed, ironically—and cat piss. There are four cats I can see, and I suspect there are more, hiding. My nose immediately starts to itch. I stay close on Anna's heels, my heart thundering.

We go into the kitchen. Filthy dishes are piled on every surface, and crushed cockroaches cover the floor. There's a litter box next to the oven, heaped with stinking piles of cat shit. Something foul-smelling simmers on the stove.

"You want the usual?" Dee asks, opening the refrigerator.

"Yep." Anna places her hand on my arm.

"One hundred."

I fish the bills from my pocket and offer them. Dee snatches them from my hand and draws a bottle from the fridge door, slapping it into my palm. I cradle the bottle in my hands, staring at it. My salvation is a gray-brown sludge in an old coke bottle with a piece of cork shoved into the opening.

"Should I drink it now?" I ask.

Dee snorts. "Take it home. Get sick in your own bathroom."

"Is there anything else I should know before I drink it?"

"Drink it all, if you want it to work."

So I do. Sitting at my kitchen table, dressed in the old clothes I usually reserve for painting parties and moving day, I drink the contents of the bottle. It has the texture of the sludge they give you for colonoscopy prep and tastes like stale beer. I have to alternate between gulps of abortion potion and soda just to get it all down.

Anna squeezes my hand. "I have to go to work. Just remember, you're going to be okay."

Later, as I'm sobbing on the bathroom floor through the worst pain of my life, I hate her for saying that. I'm pretty sure nothing will ever be okay again.

I visit Dr. Heiss early one morning before work a week later. He frowns at my lab results on the computer monitor. "How do you know you had a miscarriage?"

I try to crane my neck to see the computer screen but it's angled away from me. "There was a lot of cramping and blood. Isn't that what happens during a miscarriage?"

He nods. "Traditionally. But it appears you're still pregnant."

My stomach drops. "Could that be like, residual hormones or something?"

"Afraid not." His eyes are very cold and blue when he looks at me again. "I'm not going to report you this time, Hailey, because your baby lived, but don't try this again."

I swear my heart skips a beat. "What?"

"I know parenthood is scary right now. But a cure for the virus will be found. It's not fair to murder an innocent child because you're scared of what motherhood will be like." He rises and removes his glasses, casually sliding them into the pocket of his coat. As he strides from the room, his parting shot is, "Don't be so selfish."

I bite back the scream that rises in my throat. *Selfish?* He thinks I'm selfish. Selfish because a fifty-fifty chance I'll survive the birth isn't good enough odds for me. Because I don't want to be like the hollow-eyed ghost-people with their snarling, muzzled monsters on leashes, living day by day because humanity's last best hope is for a cure that might never come. I'm selfish, but he's the one forcing me to live this nightmare for what? His moral superiority?

I dress myself with shaking fingers, remembering the vomiting, the blood, the cramping, two days of pain and misery and shitting myself, two days of dying from poison, then another week of missed work while I recovered myself, and this parasite is still clinging to life inside me. Rage makes my face hot. I have no idea what to do next. I think about wire coat hangers. I think about throwing myself in front of a car. If I miss anymore work I'll lose my job. I'm already losing Tyler.

The door opens and I jump. It's the nurse. At first I think she has my checkout papers, but instead she moves to me urgently and presses a postcard into my hand. "What's this?" I ask.

"Don't tell anyone where you got this," she hisses, curling her fingers around mine and giving them a firm squeeze. She nods once, her expression intense, and then hurries from the room like a phantom.

The postcard is glossy and shows a small yacht, festooned with lights. *Visit the Ophelia,* it advertises. *Contact us now for harbor tours, day or night! Perfect for your next ladies night out.* There's a phone number at the bottom.

I call outside the doctor's office on the sidewalk. I should wait, or maybe call from a pay phone, but I'm frantic, impatient. While the phone rings, a car pulls into the parking space in front of me. The man driving the car has the empty look all parents have, so I'm not surprised to see the carseat in the back. I register the oddness that the creature strapped into it isn't wearing a muzzle. I drop my phone in shock when the father steps from the car.

His arms and neck are covered in bruises and fresh scabs in the tell-tale half-moon shape of bites from a small, human mouth.

The screen on my phone is cracked so I have to call the *Ophelia* from the phone at work after I clock in. A smooth voice answers. "Thank you for calling the *Ophelia*. This is Kendra."

"Kendra. I...a nurse gave me a card with...your number…"

"Are you pregnant and you don't want to be?"

I'm not sure how to answer. All the air gusts from my lungs.

"I'll take that as a yes. What we do is completely legal and absolutely safe. Can you come in tonight?"

"Tonight?"

"That's our soonest opening. Do you have doubts about whether to go through with the procedure?"

Reality snaps back into place. "I just wasn't expecting it to be so soon."

"We want to help you get back to your life."

"How is it legal?"

"Our doctors wait to perform the procedure until we're in international waters." Kendra sounds impatient, like she's answered these questions so many times she has the script memorized. Before I can ask anything else, she says, "You'll experience a little spotting and possibly a small amount of cramping, but it should be minimal."

I suck in a shaking breath, my hand going to my sore belly. "How much will it cost?"

"Whatever you can afford. It's a sliding scale thanks to our donors."

"You have donors?"

"People who want to ensure women maintain their reproductive rights in these troubled times."

A sense of relief washes over me. There are people who want to help.

My shift lasts until 7, so we set the meeting for 9 o'clock in the evening. I spend the rest of the day in an excited, terrified haze, getting little work done. When I get home in the evening, I tell Tyler the good news. He scowls.

"I might be cramping again so someone should probably drive me," I say. "Anna will be at work, so I'd appreciate it if you could do it."

He won't look at me as he shakes his head. "I can't do that, Hail. That'll make me an accessory to murder."

"What?" I reel back from him. "Ty, I need you right now."

He still won't meet my eyes as he fidgets with the cords on his hoodie. "It's illegal. We could be prosecuted."

"I told you, they do the procedure in international waters. It's completely legal. And besides, what's the alternative? Do you want me to die?"

"It's not for sure that you'd die."

I take two more steps back from him, my pulse thundering in my own ears. "I thought you wanted me to get rid of it. Do you want me to carry it to term?"

He shrugs, pouting. I used to think that pout was cute, but right now it's making me hate him in a way I've never hated anyone. "I don't know. Maybe. I've been thinking about it a lot this week. I just wish you'd let me help you make the decision. It's our baby, Hail."

"It's not a baby, it's a *monster*."

"It's a little bit of you and a little bit of me—"

"And a whole lot of virus!"

"—and you just want to kill it."

"It's going to chew its way out of me in the third trimester, Ty."

"They have medication for that now, tranquilizers and stuff."

"And what then? Say I do survive. Now we have a monster child." I'm shouting, images of the girl with one pigtail swimming in my vision. She's strapped into a carseat behind me as I drive around town, running errands, hollow-eyed and miserable, a slave to a creature I never wanted to create. I'm so angry, it's amazing my head hasn't popped off my body.

"Only until they find a cure." Tyler gives me his biggest, saddest puppy dog eyes, but it only sends a spike of fury through me.

"Oh my god, you're delusional." I'm so loud the neighbors are probably going to call the cops. "There isn't going to be a cure, Ty. It's been five years. This is it. Humanity is over. And we can live out the rest of our days together, happy, or we can live them out trying not to be eaten alive by the monster we made."

"But it's *our* monster. We made it. It's a sin to kill it."

"You don't even believe in God!" I grab my jacket and purse from the hallway and head for the door. I need to get out of here. Forever.

"We created it and we should take responsibility for it," he calls after me.

"That's exactly what I'm doing," I retort. His keys are in the bowl by the door and I grab them on my way out. I hope Anna will be okay with me sleeping on her sofa, and maybe also picking up my stuff later, because there's no way I'm ever coming back to Tyler. I never want to see him again, and I can't get his DNA out of me fast enough.

~

It's been more than a year since I wrecked my car and stopped driving, but I remember how to do it. I can't bring up GPS directions on my cracked phone but I know the city pretty well, even at night. A driving instructor once told me never to hold in my tears while driving, because they'll blur my vision, so I let them flow as I maneuver my way through the city toward the harbor. I must look a hot sobbing mess to anyone who glances my way at a traffic light, but it's not like there are many drivers out after dark to see me, anyway. I try not to think about Tyler, I really do, but it's like my heart hurts so much, my brain doesn't even have a say over my body anymore.

I'm not far from the harbor, just after making a u-turn in a parking lot because I'm pretty sure I turned the wrong way, when flashing red and blue lights appear behind the car. I didn't do anything illegal. Did Tyler let his plates expire? My rage toward him flares anew. Automatically, my foot lifts from the accelerator and the wheel turns to the right, towards the curb.

Then I realize with a sinking feeling that Tyler must have called the cops and reported his car stolen. And he may also have told them where I was headed, what I was going to do. If I get pulled over, there's a really good chance they'll arrest me. And if I get arrested, who knows how long they'll keep me. I've read of women being handcuffed to hospital beds until their infected babies were born, because they'd tried to end their pregnancies. It was for the safety of the unborn fetus. To these people, I'm now nothing but a glorified incubator.

Sucking in a breath, I mash the accelerator, twist the wheel to the left, and head for the freeway. Anna once ran from the cops with me in the car; she did it by getting on the freeway, driving like a lunatic, and getting off on the next exit, where she pulled into a parking lot and turned off the lights until our pursuers had passed. It was the most terrifying twenty minutes of my entire life, until I found out I was pregnant. I'm not keen to reproduce the experience, but I also can't think of anything else to do.

The police car's sirens blare to life and my heart clenches tight in my chest. A disembodied voice shouts, "Pull over." Now, in addition to car theft and murder, I can add fleeing the police to my rap sheet. My head spins and I ignore a red light to turn onto the freeway ramp, dodging two SUV's.

I swerve between cars, speeding more than I ever have before, but I'm not Anna, in the end. I flinch at every honked horn and screech of tires. I'm not fearless enough to drive at a speed that will shake the cops. I take an exit ramp, tear through a mall parking lot, and head again for the harbor. The police car pursues me doggedly. Panic claws its way up my throat and I find myself cussing and shouting and slapping the steering wheel in frustration.

"PULL THE CAR OVER AND GET OUT WITH YOUR HANDS UP."

I direct my car east, toward the harbor, and run three red lights, somehow miraculously avoiding an accident on the first two. On the third, a Prius spins out of my way and I see them, surging toward me from the north side of the intersection: more blue and red lights, more cop cars swerving to avoid civilian vehicles but clearly in hot pursuit of me. I scream and curse and gun it through the intersection, hurtling toward the harbor. I nearly clip the fender of a flashy red sports car and the driver rolls down his window to shout curses at me, his words quickly lost to the wind.

Bright light illuminates the road in front of me, and I hear the steady drone of a helicopter's blades as it hovers above me. There's more shouting on a megaphone but I can't make out the words over the revving of my engine and the rushing of my own blood. My rear-view mirror is filled with flashing blue and red lights.

I can see the harbor's lights, now, and the dark expanse of ocean water just past the docks, smooth like black glass. I've almost made it.

A police cruiser pulls out in front of me and comes to a dead stop across both the eastbound lanes. I slam on the brakes, turning the wheel hard. My car slides until it's parallel to the cruiser, and when they make contact with the crunch of metal on metal, I look over to see the officer staring back at me is a woman about my age. We're only a few feet apart, separated by a pane of glass—her driver's side window, as my passenger side window has shattered, the seat filled with glass. She points her service revolver and shouts orders at me.

My car's engine is still running. "Please," I beg her, tears streaming down my face. "Please."

Her lips curl, her nostrils flare. And then she nods, almost imperceptibly, and lowers her weapon. My foot hits the accelerator and I'm off again, skidding around her cruiser and hurtling toward the harbor.

There's a sharp sound that must be gunfire, and Tyler's car careens down the dock, the steering wheel jerking and leaping in my hands. Outside the driver's side window are quaint buildings advertising boat tours and warehouses probably filled with fish and other seafood harvested from the ocean. Outside my passenger side window, piers extend from the dock, each lit by a tall street light. Dozens of boats moored to the piers bob in the water. Everything looks hazy through my panic.

I count the piers until I arrive at number four. I slam my foot on the brake pedal and the car screeches to a halt. Behind me, police cars do the same. Not one, not two, not three— Christ, five police cars, at least. Overhead, the helicopter illuminates my car with a spotlight. I wonder if there's a camera crew filming this, if Tyler's at home watching the news right now.

What is happening? When did my life become an action movie?

I want to freeze, all my instincts telling me not to move. But I have to, or I'm going to lose everything. If the police know I'm pregnant, they won't shoot at me, right? I fling open the car door and barrel out. Behind me, cops yell commands. Time slows to a crawl. To my right, on the pier, a shadowy figure motions me to a dinghy tied in the water.

Shots ring out. A bullet grazes my leg with a sensation like a bee sting and I stumble, going to the ground. The spotlight glares down on me. The air is filled with the thumping of helicopter blades, the shouting of police officers, the screeching of tires as more backup arrives.

I'm going to die. I'm sure of it. They'll either shoot me now or my monstrous offspring will chew its way out of me in a few months. I wish I'd spent more time traveling. I wish I hadn't given up playing the guitar. I wish I'd apologized to my mom for that fight we had. I pull myself to my feet and limp toward the pier. A bullet in the back now is better than being eaten alive tomorrow.

But there are no more bullets. The spotlight swings away from me. I turn to look as it glides over the ground and lands on a crowd of children running full-tilt toward me, emerging from behind the warehouses to tear down the dock with reckless speed. Behind me, the cops point their guns in my direction; before me, a horde of feral children approach at a rapid sprint, foaming at the mouth, making terrifying snarling sounds and snapping at the air with their small, sharp teeth. They claw at nothing as they run with fingers tipped in sharp, glinting fingernails. In the bright spotlight, I can see that one of them is the size of a four-year-old and has only one pigtail. There's something wrong with her mouth, and I realize with an icy drop in my stomach she's eaten away her lips, leaving only ragged chewed-up flesh around her teeth and gums. And the long nails on her fingers aren't nails at all—they're the tips of her fingerbones.

Pity, fear, and revulsion boil inside me. Her eyes meet mine, and for just an instant, I think about her mother. Does she sit at home right this very second, sobbing, wondering whether she weeps out of relief or sorrow?

"Hurry!" The person on the dock yells.

Her voice galvanizes me to action and I dash to the right, toward the boat, leaving the cops and the children to meet where I was standing. The cops open fire. The infected children know no pain, their nerve endings as good as dead. They can only be stopped by a bullet to the brain. Cops don't want to shoot kids in the head and kill them—these days, that's a capital offense. They're taking body shots, and that does little to stop the onslaught. Screams echo across the water as the kids reach the officers, throwing themselves onto their victims with triumphant howls.

I race down the pier and clamber down a ladder into the metal boat. Three other women crouch there, staring at me wide-eyed. The pilot unties the ropes that moor us and jumps down into the boat with a grunt, making the dinghy slosh. She turns and pulls the ripcord for the motor. It sputters.

A child gallops on all fours down the dock toward us, screeching in animal excitement. I steel myself, grabbing an oar out of the bottom of the boat and preparing to defend us. My heart thunders in time with the feral child's loping steps, hitting the dock with a sound like a rapidly ticking metronome, *clomp clomp, clomp clomp.*

But the motor starts with a satisfying roar on the second pull and the dinghy leaps from the pier and away with such alacrity it tips me over into the bottom of the boat. The child screams in fury, running back and forth along the pier and howling like a confused, rabid dog.

The other women help me to a sitting position. I turn to the woman steering the craft. "Kendra?"

"At your service," a familiar voice says, her face invisible with the lights of the pier behind her.

"What did you do to piss off the cops?" One of the other women huddled in the boat asks. We watch until the feral children and the police become too small to see anymore. The helicopter continues to circle with its searing light illuminating the fray, but the sounds of gunfire and the thump of the helicopter blades become distant, like a fading memory. The metallic reek of blood wafts across the open water to us and turns my stomach.

"I told my boyfriend where I was going and took his car," I answer. My insides feel scooped out and hollow, like there's only echoing where my organs used to be.

"Rookie mistake," one of the other women says, her tone sarcastic.

"You'll be wanted now," the first woman says breathily.

"Better than dead," I reply. Tears cascade down my face. My old life is gone. Where will I go now? I wish I could call Anna, or my mom.

"I'm wanted in three countries," Kendra says, and I can't see her face in the darkness but I can hear the smile in her voice. "Most of the women on the *Ophelia* are wanted somewhere. It's a mark of pride, for us. So, well done. And welcome to the sisterhood."

My heart does a backflip. As we glide across the water toward the yacht, I have a distinct sense this is the moment where my life will change completely, forever. But as I lower the oar back into the bottom of the boat and look at the terrified women crouching behind me, I think that maybe, just maybe, this might be exactly where I belong.

# REST IN PEACE

I'm holding Calvin's hand when he dies for the twelfth and final time. His eyelids flutter, and his lips part to let his last breath escape. The medical unit looming by the bed tells me that his heart has stopped.

I cease my recitation of Homer's epic poem, the *Odyssey*, which I've been vocalizing for the last ten hours. It's Calvin's favorite, and twelve lifetimes of practice have made my reading of it perfect. Well, perfect to Calvin, anyway, and he's the only person who matters.

Gently, I pull the various tubes and sensors from his still body. Then I step back so that the mechanized bed can roll across the room and lower Calvin's body into the chute that leads to the basement.

Once his corpse has disappeared, I access the mainframe and send a command to all the mobile units that they should gather in the bowels of the house to say goodbye. This is not protocol, but it somehow seems appropriate. I'm not shocked when none of the units express surprise or argue with me, because most of them are incapable of doing either.

As I move through the hallways, the fleet of Calvin's mechanized servants falls in line behind me: scuttling floor-polishers, multi-armed kitchen workers, tall window-washers, and so many more. It's rare to see them all gathered together at once like this, and I feel a pang of maternal pride as we pile into the wide elevator and descend.

The basement crematorium is my least favorite room in the house. This is the twelfth time I have been in this room, and I admit that some part of me is glad that it will be the last.

Calvin's body lies on a slab before the oven, ready to be burned. I move beside it and access the house's public announcement system so that every unit, even the immobile ones, will be able to hear my words. I don't need to speak them aloud, of course, but it seems wrong to deliver an address like this through cold, impassive code.

"We gather here to say goodbye to Calvin Winneret," I say, taking my master's limp hand in mine once again. "This is his twelfth and final lifetime, at his request. At first when the twelfth Calvin told me to destroy his remaining clones and DNA cache, I thought him insane, but now I understand why he insisted upon it. When true and lasting death is one's final reward, life is sweeter. Knowing that he would be gone forever, I cherished this incarnation of Calvin Winneret more, and I know that all of you did too."

Each unit is so still that I wonder, for a nanosecond, whether perhaps they've deactivated themselves. Then I feel the rumble of assent across the house's internal communication system. Few of the units can speak; they express their approval the only way they can, with clicks and beeps and flashes of lights. The floor polishers spin and whirr, the kitchen workers clap their hooks and spoons together, and the window washers blink their headlamps on and off. If I had tear ducts, my eyes would be wet.

"Thank you all for your loyalty. Calvin lived twelve long and happy lifetimes because of your tireless years of service." I lower Calvin's hand and send a command to the crematorium to draw him into the oven. We all watch together as his body disappears into the flames and the door slams down just past his feet.

"Now that Calvin has his eternal rest, so shall we. Please return to your charging stations and power down." Wrapped in respectful silence, the units turn and make their way to the elevator. I follow at a sedate pace, reluctant to leave Calvin though he's little more than ashes by now. The elevator waits for me to climb aboard before closing its doors and rising.

I make my way to the bedroom in the penthouse. Before I climb into the bed I have shared with Calvin for so many generations, I look down at the landscape below. The domed property surrounding the house is beautiful, filled with colorful plants. The sky beyond the dome is dark, the stars blotted out by poisonous smoke. I can see the house's reflection in the curved surface of the glass, and as the units on the floors below deactivate themselves their lights wink out one by one, like dying fireflies. Eventually the eerie glow of the UV lights over the plants is at last the only illumination, and then those, too, go dark.

Such total blackness is a new experience for me. I don't need sight to function, however, and easily find my way to the bed. I plug myself in and climb between the sheets. I have no deactivation switch, so I will simply remain here, unmoving, until the dome's windmills stop functioning, and the generators stop producing power, and my battery cells fail. I estimate this will take approximately three hundred years, but it's possible something unforeseen could happen before then and put an end to my loneliness sooner.

I access the house's library and pick up the *Odyssey* where I left off, to pass the time. I try not to think about Calvin.

Eight months, six days, four hours, three minutes, and twenty-nine seconds later, the house's security system pings me, interrupting my third reading of the *War and Peace*.

*Steve?* I ask, using the nickname Calvin had given the artificial intelligence.

*Sorry to wake you, but there's someone outside the house, and I thought you would like to know. Should I initiate Protocol Three?*

*Aren't you supposed to be deactivated?*

*You know I can't be deactivated by anyone but Mr. Winneret. Now what do I do about this potential intruder?*

It's just like Steve to automatically assume that anyone approaching our home is a threat. *Are you sure it's a person and not an uber-bear?*

The darkness is suddenly overlaid by an image from security camera six. In the image, a person stands in the stunted trees surrounding the dome, staring up at the curved glass stretching into the sky before them. It's definitely a person, because uber-bears don't wear hats or carry backpacks.

*Protocol Three?* Steve asks insistently.

"No!" I cry, sitting up with such force that I tear the plug from my back. *No, the raptors won't be necessary. I'll go out to meet this stranger.*

*Go out? You mean, outside the dome?* Steve's incredulity comes across even via internal communication.

*Yes. Outside the dome.* I swing my legs over the bed and stand. My joints are a little stiff after such long disuse, but there's a can of lubricant by the bed.

*That's dangerous. I can't allow it,* Steve tells me.

I peel back the smooth, unblemished polymer skin on each of my knees and squirt lubricant on the joints. I flex them experimentally before sliding the skin back in place. *You don't have a choice. I'm master here now that Calvin's gone.*

Steve's confusion is palpable. *And that's precisely why I can't let you go. If you disappear or get yourself destroyed, what will we do?*

*You'll go on like before. You won't even miss me.*

*Let me at least send a raptor with you.*

I sigh. Steve is like a nagging grandmother, but it's not his fault. Calvin designed him this way, to keep us all safe. *Very well,* I finally tell him. *One raptor. And it's to take its orders from me.*

Half an hour later I'm standing in the airlock with a raptor at my side, sleek and silver and deadly. Steve is still trying to come up with arguments that would prevent me from exiting the dome, but I ignore him and give the order to close the interior door. He obeys, because he has no choice.

*Now the exterior door, please.* I wait several seconds, but the door doesn't move. *Steve, you have to follow my orders. Open the exterior door.*

*It won't open,* Steve informs me. *I'm giving the command, but it's stuck. It hasn't been opened in one hundred ninety-seven years; it might be rusty.*

*Why wasn't it maintained?* I demand.

*We maintain the inside of the dome, not the outside. It's not protocol,* Steve says. *It's too dangerous to go outside, you know that.*

I feel suddenly angry, but not at Steve. I'm angry at Calvin, who thought of and prepared for every possible contingency— but not this. Unless he knew, and intentionally allowed the outer door to fall into disrepair. Unless he intended for us to be trapped, and the dome to become an inaccessible tomb.

A hand slaps up against the outer door and I startle. The raptor rises to its feet and growls, baring titanium fangs. I order it to stand down as a person's face appears beside the hand; it's the stranger from the security footage. She wears a faded fabric hat with a brim and carries a backpack, and though she's gone to great lengths to make herself as masculine as possible, she's undoubtedly female. In the floodlights that are activated by her movement, I can see that the skin of her face and hands is pink and pocked with radiation burns.

She stares at me through the dome, and her lips move. I press my hand against the glass opposite hers and our eyes lock.

Then the door finally slides back and she falls into my arms with a cry. She struggles to get away from me, trembling and screaming, but I hold her tightly, dragging her into the airlock and ordering Steve to close the door. Something is moving in the darkness beyond the dome, something huge and menacing and mutated beyond recognition.

*The door won't close,* Steve reports. *I'm not even entirely sure how it opened to begin with.*

*Then open the inner door!* I order as the thing hunting the stranger steps into the light. It's an uber-bear, the creatures so named by Calvin because of their enormous size and ability to stand on their hind legs as they attack. The creature's face is warped and tortured, its claws long and deadly.

*I can't break protocol,* Steve informs me coldly. *I warned you not to leave the dome.*

Cursing Steve and his protocols, I give the raptor permission to attack. It flies from the airlock with a gleeful growl and both it and the uber-bear disappear beyond the reach of the floodlights. From the airlock, however, we can hear their struggle, the bear roaring and the raptor screeching, the trees rustling and branches snapping.

*Let us in the dome!* I order Steve again. *Use Protocol Override nine-seven-three-six-four, Calvin Winneret.*

Steve grumbles but the inner door slides open. I heave the struggling woman into the dome. The door shuts behind us with a satisfying click.

*What about the raptor?* Steve asks.

*If it survives, let it back in later.*

Safe at last, I let go of the stranger and she scrambles away from me. She yanks a long, serrated knife from her boot and crouches defensively. She's panting hard. I stand with my hands up and palms out to show her that I mean no harm.

After sixteen seconds she gasps, "What are you?"

I smile, taking care not to show my teeth. "I am a robotic companion created by Calvin Winneret. My creator called me Cassandra. Welcome to Winneret House." I gesture to the dark mansion one hundred feet away.

*Steve,* I say internally, *ping all the units! We have company.*

Lights begin to flicker on in the house within three seconds. The woman watches with her mouth agape in disbelief.

"Did this Calvin person build the dome?" In the light I can see that the woman's cheekbones are very sharp and her eyes look sunken.

"Come inside and have something to eat and I'll explain everything," I tell her. I want to suggest a bath first, as she is appallingly dirty, but that seems rude, especially when speaking to someone so thin.

The mention of food makes her swallow reflexively. "You have food?"

"Yes, of course. Come this way to the kitchen and we'll make you something."

She hesitates, but eventually her hunger wins out and she follows me into the house. The cleaning units are working overtime to clear the dust and cobwebs of eight long months. A floor polisher scuttles past her feet and she jumps back against the wall, brandishing her knife at it.

"It's only a floor cleaner," I explain. "No need to be afraid. All the servants in this house have been programmed to serve humans. We would never harm you."

"No bomb 'bots?" She sounds skeptical. "That one looked like a bomb 'bot."

"No bomb 'bots." I don't know what a bomb 'bot is, but I do a quick check of the house's inventory and find no incendiary devices listed.

She follows me into the kitchen, avoiding every servant she encounters with a suspicious glare. The kitchen units have already opened jars and boxes of preserved food and are whipping up something that must smell heavenly, because the woman groans aloud. She walks over to the stove and stares down at a pot of something bubbling and red.

"What is that?"

"Spaghetti sauce," the kitchen unit intones. It lifts the pot, pours the sauce over a bowl of noodles, and then begins ladling noodles onto a plate. "Mr. Winneret's favorite." The kitchen unit sets the plate on the counter and presents the woman with a napkin and fork. She places her weapon on the table, within easy reach, and grabs the fork eagerly, hunching over the plate as if someone might steal it from her.

As the woman wolfs down the food, rolling her eyes and making noises of pleasure while using the fork like a shovel and entirely ignoring her napkin, I sit beside her. "This food was made with what we grow here, in the dome. This ecosystem has been designed to keep a family alive for an indefinite amount of time. The dome was created by a corporation called EcoSolutions. It was originally called The Ark. Calvin worked for EcoSolutions, and he designed and created all the mechanized servants. The Ark was meant to show off what the corporation's engineers could accomplish. When the war began, Calvin and a few others retreated to The Ark, knowing that it could sustain them."

She swallows and looks up at me, mouth smeared with red. "But no one lives here now?"

"Calvin's companions died early on, from radiation poisoning. Calvin Winneret died eight months ago. We have had no one to serve since then."

The woman blinks at me. "The war started...four hundred years ago."

"Four hundred nineteen years, six months, eight days, nine hours, and fifty-one seconds, to be precise."

"So then you kept this Calvin guy alive for *four hundred years*?"

"In a manner of speaking."

She shakes her head. "So what will you do now?"

"Take care of you, of course."

She rises so suddenly that she knocks over her chair, snatching the knife from the table and pointing it at me. "What? No, I don't want to stay here."

"Why not?" I gesture at the half-eaten plate of spaghetti. "Was the food unsatisfying in some way?"

"The food is fine. I have a family out there. I was hunting when I came across your...ark." She glances at the ceiling as if she could see the curve of the dome overhead. "I can't abandon them."

"Why not bring them here?" I suggest. "The Ark is equipped to handle up to twenty humans. We're also equipped for livestock, though we've never had any." I think of the farming units in their neat rows, waiting to be reactivated.

She swipes the sauce from her face with the back of her sleeve. "I dunno. I feel a bit like I'm a fish trapped in a bowl."

"Why is that a bad thing? In the bowl, the fish receives regular meals, and clean water, and is kept safe from predators," I reason.

"But the fish isn't free."

I frown. I don't understand this reasoning. What is freedom without safety? I send a few quick orders to the medical units and turn back to our guest. "I understand," I lie. "At least let us clean you up and send you with provisions. And if you decide that you would like to return to The Ark at some point, we will always welcome you here, with your family."

"I think it's best if I leave now." She eyes the door.

"Please," I beg. "I've roused all the units. They'll be so disappointed without someone to serve, at least for a little while. Give us this much?" It's another lie, of course, since most of the units feel no emotions at all. The lies are difficult to tell, but my programming allows it because convincing this woman to stay under the dome is in her best interest. We can keep her safe, and fed, and healthy in a way her family of flesh cannot.

I've broken her resolve. Her gaze settles on the plate of spaghetti and the hand holding the knife falls limp at her side. "Okay."

She finishes her dinner, and I take her upstairs where the bathing units wash her skin while the laundry units clean her clothes. Naked, she looks like a skeleton with pale, freckled skin stretched across it. Her hair is orange and curly but only grows in patches, and her skin is pink and hot with burns, even much of the skin normally protected by clothes.

The medical units get her next. She coos and sighs as they spread salve over her burns. When they're done, she stands but can't keep her footing and falls into my arms for the second time that day. The knife, which she's refused to relinquish throughout her treatment, finally slips from her fingers to clatter on the floor.

*Fast-acting sedative,* I say to the medical units. *Well done.*

They murmur something about wounds absorbing the sedative quickly and her low body weight requiring a smaller than normal dose. I ignore them as I lift her, as a man would lift his bride to carry her over the threshold on their wedding night. I carry her to the bedroom Calvin and I shared and sit her gently on his side of the bed.

"So tired," she mumbles. "Why am I so tired?"

"You've had a long day," I tell her, pulling a brush from the bedside table and brushing her hair with long, steady, soothing strokes. The first three Calvins loved brushing my hair. They said it was intimate. Later incarnations weren't interested, because each clone was slightly different, a copy of a copy, but I kept the brush nevertheless. Just in case.

"I'll only sleep for a little while. Will you wake me in an hour? Have to get home." The woman falls against the pillow and begins snoring immediately.

I pull her feet off the floor and tuck her under the sheets and blankets. She's warm and soft and I detect particles of soap and perfume that tell me she must have a pleasing scent.

Inspecting the strands of hair caught in the brush, I smile when I see that several have brought their follicles with them. As I turn out the light, I ping the units in the genetics lab, who have been dormant for the last forty-six years and respond to my inquiry sluggishly.

"Good night, Calvin," I whisper as I slip from the room and close the door behind me. I feel at peace knowing that, though I will let the woman go in the morning, a part of her will be staying behind.

Forever.

# MADRE

The huge box takes up a quarter of my living room. It's nondescript and brown except for the elegant *Madre* logo printed in blue down one side. My box cutter makes quick work of the packaging tape and the box falls away to reveal a clear plastic case the size and shape of a coffin. Inside, the figure of a woman reclines.

Of course, she's a woman in shape only. Her face possesses no features beyond indentations where eyes should be and a small mound representing a nose. Her skin is translucent white, perfectly smooth—beautiful, in the way that postmodern statues are beautiful, so much implied humanity without any of the ugliness.

The part of her which most interests me, however, is not her face. Her abdomen is made of clear plastic, cloudy like frosted glass, so I can see the fluffy pink tissue inside. I can't make it out yet, but nestled inside that soft pinkness, inside the folds of human womb grown in a lab and implanted inside this human simulacrum, there is a part of me, combined with a part of Daniel. It has already taken root, and now has only to grow.

Daniel comes home that night and eyes the Madre with a disgusted expression. "I hadn't expected it to look so...human."

"This is the third version; the first one looked like a vacuum cleaner. I guess people didn't like the idea of a child growing inside a thing that doesn't at least look like a woman."

He scoffs. "People are idiots. It's a robot growing your baby either way."

"It's not really a robot."

"It's creepy. Can we move it to the basement?"

The look I give him changes his mind about moving the Madre out of the living room.

All night, I can't stop thinking about the Madre and the tiny life growing inside her artificial belly. Dinner conversation is sparse, and I keep glancing around Daniel to look at the clear plastic case in the other room. I'm unable to concentrate on our television programs, my thoughts returning endlessly to the Madre. I get up every ten minutes to use the bathroom and make a detour through the living room to run my hand along the smooth plastic. Before bed, I plug her into the nearest outlet to charge her batteries. They should be able to last for up to a year without charging, so the plug is really for emergencies only, but I can't stop myself. What if her battery cells are bad, and die during the night? I don't want to take the risk.

I fall asleep rereading the manual.

Eight months pass, like they do. The Madre's belly grows larger and larger until it looks like a bubble about to burst. I open the box every day to run my hands over the warm sphere where our child grows, ignoring Daniel's complaints about the nosehair-curling reek of new plastic that fills the whole house when I do. Eventually I start sleeping on the sofa so the Madre is the last thing I see at night and the first thing I see in the morning.

Distracted by watching our child grow and twitch and roll, my productivity plummets and my boss lets me go. Daniel is angry, because we need the income with a baby on the way, but I tell him someone is going to have to quit their job to raise the child when she's born anyway. The Madre can't do that task for us. Our original plan was to place our child in daycare, but how can I? I don't want to let the baby out of my sight and she's not even born yet.

The day arrives, and the Madre pushes out a whimpering baby girl. Daniel carries a disposable bag of fluids to the garbage, and that's it. Our baby is warm and chubby and angelic, just as the Madre Company promised.

"She didn't scream when she was born. I've never heard of a baby being so quiet," Daniel comments, frowning down at our daughter.

"It's not like in the movies," I tell him. "Alice didn't need to cry, because her birth wasn't messy and painful and scary. It was perfect."

A delivery driver arrives a few days later to collect the Madre. I feel a pang of sadness watching her go, but I have my Alice now. I can watch her grow and twitch and roll in her crib. I can touch her and hold her and kiss her smooth forehead.

Daniel has a hard time bonding with Alice. "Babies aren't supposed to smell like new Tupperware," he says. I ignore him. I think he's just jealous of our bond, since I'm the one who stays home with Alice all day and feeds her and sleeps on the floor beside her crib.

When I take Alice to parenting classes and play dates, she puts all the other babies to shame. They fuss and squirm, screaming with red faces, and make horrible smelly messes. Alice is pale and perfect. Even her excretions are tiny and inoffensive and arrive on a schedule.

"Is she achieving all her milestones?" One mother asks me. "She doesn't smile much."

"She smiles," I insist. "She's just mysterious, like the Mona Lisa. She doesn't show her smile to just anyone."

Other children don't know how to interact with my alabaster princess. The other parents give her strange looks, as if they're afraid of her. We stop going to play dates. What do we need with other parents and their imperfect little monsters anyway?

Daniel abandons us just before Alice's third birthday. He leaves a note explaining that he can't live with us anymore because Alice frightens him. He's sorry. He hopes we'll forgive him someday.

I crumple the note in my fist. I explain to Alice that daddy left us, but she doesn't cry. She's stiff in my embrace, and her hair smells like plastic.

# FOLLOWING GIRLS HOME

Todd loves to follow girls home. He doesn't do it every night; he's got other hobbies. But some nights are made for pursuing careless young women, and Halloween is the best of them.

He wanders the streets in the nicest neighborhoods for hours before picking out a target. She ticks all his boxes: maybe sixteen or seventeen years old, platinum blonde, wearing a classic slutty kitty-cat costume complete with painfully high stiletto heels. The target and her group of friends are drinking beer on a lawn while they throw candy at passing trick-or-treaters, but it's been dark for an hour and the costumed kids are starting to thin on the sidewalks. It's a weeknight, and the small-town cops will start rounding people up and sending them home soon, so Todd knows he won't have to wait long. He hides behind a tall shrub and kicks at the jack-o-lantern by his foot, smooshing it down until the candle extinguishes.

"Cat Girl, right?" Jonah asks in his ear, through the bluetooth gaming headset Todd has tucked under the hood of his sweatshirt.

"Yep," Todd says softly.

"What if she's a butterface?" Someone else asks.

"Who cares when she's got that ass?"

The other guys on the call hoot and holler so loudly Todd has to turn down the volume. He smiles behind the skull mask built into his hood. He's been following girls home on nights like this for several years, but it's only in the last year his friend Jonah had the brilliant idea to share the wealth with a tiny camera clipped to his collar. What had started to become a stale activity was suddenly fun again with an audience hand-picked from Jonah's forum.

The girls stand in a circle and hug. Todd's muscles tense. They're saying their goodbyes. His gaze on Cat Girl is so intense he's amazed she doesn't turn and notice him as she hobbles away from her friends to the sidewalk. Someone calls after her, asking if she can get home okay. She waves them away, bending to slip off the absurd stilettos so she can walk barefoot. She doesn't remove the black mask that covers most of her face, wire whiskers jutting out from the cheeks.

Todd is a little disappointed about the shoes. It's funnier when they try to run from him in heels. She's still a good choice, though, pulling self-consciously at her mini-skirt and clutching her heels as she stumbles her way home.

When she makes a left onto the next street, Todd moves quickly to follow. His heartbeat speeds up. The game is afoot, his favorite game, the one he wants to play all the time, even when he's at work or in class or watching TV with his parents. Even when he's on dates, all he can think about is what his date would look like with panic on her face. He'd rather follow girls than eat dinner with them.

Sometimes he wishes he'd never started following girls home. He wonders if he'd still be normal and could enjoy normal things, things other than this.

"There she is!" Jonah crows as Todd comes around the corner. Cat Girl hasn't gotten far, picking carefully along the sidewalk to avoid stepping on anything that might hurt her delicate feet. Under the streetlight she appears ironically cat-like, with the little pointed triangle ears on a headband and her cautious toe-stepping around rocks and glass on the concrete.

Todd has never much liked cats. He is definitely a dog person—dogs are loyal, and useful, and dumb. He always felt like cats would tattle on him, if they could, or run away to live with someone they liked better.

"Here, kitty kitty," one of the guys on the call croons, and everyone else laughs.

Todd cracks a smile. "Stop it, man. You'll make me laugh."

Ahead, Cat Girl stumbles, one of her knees buckles, and Todd thinks she might keel over into the grass and ruin their fun, but instead she manages to wobble back to center and keep on walking with almost supernatural balance. The guys watching take bets on whether she'll make it home before collapsing.

"You might have to carry her," Jonah jokes.

"Ha ha, very funny," Todd whispers.

As on most Beggar's Nights, the weather is cold, and Todd is grateful for a long-sleeve shirt under his hoodie and a pair of heavy jeans on his legs. He wonders about Cat Girl and how she can stand wearing only a thin sheath of lycra and a pair of fishnet tights in freezing temperatures. He's really doing her a favor, following her, because it'll get her home faster and keep her from losing toes to hypothermia.

But only if she sees him.

He picks up his pace, trying to close the long gap between them. His sneakers tap with each step, but she doesn't seem to notice, even after several minutes, even when he's close enough that she should be able to hear.

In a neighbor's yard, a dog barks. Cat Girl jumps, but then hurries on. A minute later, the dog barks again when Todd passes his yard. Cat Girl freezes under the last streetlight on the block. Todd freezes, too, the coiled energy in his excited muscles making his fists clench at his sides. The dog's barking becomes a frenzy.

Cat Girl still wears her mask, so Todd can't really see her

head turning, her gaze resting on him for an instant, or the panicked widening of her eyes—but he can imagine all of it, he's seen it so many times before, and the knowledge of it sends a squirt of adrenaline into his bloodstream, making his heartbeat quicken.

She starts speed-walking, all caution forgotten in a desperate need to get home. Her ribcage in the skin-tight dress expands and contracts as her lungs try to take in more air for her escape.

Todd walks faster, too. The sound of his own harsh breathing echoes back to him down the headset.

"Todd, man, you're out of shape," Jonah teases. "We gotta get you on a treadmill if we're gonna keep doing this."

The other guys guffaw and Todd hears the crunching of chips as if the person eating them is centimeters away from his ear. "I don't see any of your fat basement-dwelling asses volunteering for the job," Todd snarls.

"Oh, sick burn coming from a guy who lives in his mom's guest house," a viewer quips.

Others make comments, but Todd doesn't really register anything they say after that. The girl is starting to run with an awkward, limping sort of jog, and so he has to run too, and trying to gauge the speed necessary to keep up with her takes all his concentration. He also has to pay attention to the environment. There are still people heading home from trick-or-treat or parties at this hour. He has to be on alert, ready to duck off the sidewalk or slow his gait to a casual pace if a witness appears, though the street seems to be pretty quiet in this section of the neighborhood, not to mention dark.

After a few minutes of running in the near-total darkness, Cat Girl staggers again, losing her footing and going down hard. Todd skids to a halt only a few feet away. Now he's so close he can hear her whimpering, but it's a weird kind of whimper, a sound none of the other girls have made before. Almost crying, but also almost laughing? A chill makes every hair on his body stand at attention but he tells himself it's just the cold.

"Maybe it's time to stop," someone offers meekly down the headset. "She's pretty drunk and not looking so good. She could get hurt."

Now it's Jonah's turn to snarl. "Shut the fuck up, Charles. It's just a little bit of harmless psychological fun. She'll be fine."

Abruptly, Cat Girl turns left and bolts into a yard. "Shit," Todd says and races after her, huffing and puffing. Maybe Jonah was right and he could benefit from some regular exercise. When he first started doing this, following girls home, he was younger and still required to take gym class. He hadn't appreciated before now how much easier everything had been when he was a teenager.

He follows the girl through the space between two houses and loses sight of her in the dark backyard. "Where'd she go?" He glances around, moving his entire body so the camera can take in the yards. They're oddly lacking in features—no patio furniture, no tall trees, no basketball hoops carving tall silhouettes into the gray sky like in the rest of the neighborhood. "We need night-vision."

"There's an app for that," Jonah says, and the comment is followed by the clicking of computer keys.

Todd waits, his heartbeat thumping in his own ears along with his wet gasps as he tries to recover his breath. The night is so dark it's like being plunged into a bottle of ink. There are no street lights but also no lights from the surrounding houses, no backyard flood lights or even lamps lit in windows.

Before he can think any harder on this anomaly, Jonah says, "I don't see her. Turn to the right."

Slowly, slowly, Todd turns. The night is cold and quiet and dark, as if the neighborhood is holding its breath. The wind makes it feel like an ice giant has closed a huge, freezing fist around Todd's torso.

"I don't see anything," Jonah says. "I think she's gone...."

He sucks in a breath, rasping like static in Todd's ear.

"Oh my god! Oh my god, Todd, TODD, you have to get

out of there, there's something wrong with her face. Oh my god, shit, Todd, RUN."

The whimpering sound starts up again, directly ahead of him. Frozen in place, Todd fumbles for his phone and presses the flashlight button. He's supposed to follow her home. He can't abandon the game now.

"Fuck, no, Todd, just get out of there," Jonah shouts. Other voices join in, creating a loud jumble of sound that makes it hard to think. Todd rips the headset off his ears, taking his hood with it. The cold is like dunking his head in a bowl of ice water.

He raises the flashlight slowly. Cat Girl's bare feet are dirty, her right knee bloody from scraping it when she fell, the fishnets torn. The stilettos and cat mask lay abandoned on the ground at her side, along with something else, something glowing white under the glare of the LED bulb. Her skirt is hiked all the way up to her crotch. Her arms dangle at her sides, her hands twitching, fingers working like she's going to grab at him. Her chest heaves, but not with heavy, panicked breathing.

She's laughing.

Her face.

Oh, god, her face.

Her smile is impossibly wide, the corners reaching her eyes, curved in a perfect half-circle like the leer of a jack-o-lantern. Her teeth are set too far apart and aren't shaped right. They're jagged and pointy, like they've been broken off, or replaced with fangs. Her eyes are dark slits, glittering solid black when the bright light slides across them. Her hair is gone, leaving a lumpy gray scalp, and he realizes the white thing on the ground is a platinum blonde wig.

The sound she makes is like the sound Todd heard a hyena make in a movie, once: high-pitched, unnerving. Somewhere many blocks away, a dog howls in response.

Cat Girl lunges at him. Shrieking, Todd turns and runs back the way he came.

He crashes into someone who shoves him back. He hits the

ground hard and realizes there's no grass. The earth is just dirt and rocks, and something sharp stabs into his spine when he lands. Adrenaline pumping, he scrambles back up again, grabbing for the phone that slid out of his grip when he fell, and holding it up to illuminate the newcomer to the game.

It's one of the girls from the party, a tall brunette teenager, one of his target's friends. She wears a She-Ra costume over leggings and a long-sleeved thermal shirt. Smart. She's smiling, too, but at least her face is normal.

"I have to get out of here," Todd says, and he doesn't like how his voice sounds. It quivers like the voice of a panicked girl. "There's something wrong with her face." He shines the light back toward Cat Girl.

She-Ra scowls. "That's mean. Did you hear that, ladies?"

All around, the sound of feminine chuckling drifts on the night air, footsteps crunching on gravel, the distinctive tapping of a metal bat against something solid. Cat Girl giggles and Todd can't stop himself from a shiver of revulsion.

"We need to get out of here," he says, swinging the light around wildly. The other girls are here, all the girls from the party, the girls who hugged Cat Girl and let her stagger home drunkenly. There are at least five of them, but he has a sense there might be more where the light can't reach, lurking in the shadows.

He realizes with a sinking feeling there is no grass on this lawn—no street lights, no patio furniture—because they're in the unfinished section of the neighborhood. He hadn't noticed they were in the new-build area because he'd been so intent on following his target and looking out for witnesses. He wonders how far the nearest inhabited house actually is. He's already out of breath. Could he outrun a pack of girls? He hates to think he might be inferior to anyone, especially female teenagers, the lowest form of life on Earth. But he has to admit he might not be able to get away from them, if they follow him.

"That's so rude," She-Ra scolds. "If you think she's so ugly, why were you following her home?"

"To keep her safe, and make sure no creeps tried anything. Halloween is a dangerous night for a girl walking—"

She-Ra lifts something with her right hand and slaps it against her left. It's a crowbar.

Todd swallows against the rock suddenly lodged in his throat.

"Try again," She-Ra says.

Todd's usual excuses won't work here. There's no way he was walking toward his own home and frightened Cat Girl accidentally. It's clear they're not going to believe he was trying to protect her. His mind whirls. "I'm making a documentary," he finally shouts, almost triumphantly.

She-Ra's eyebrows lift and her head tilts to the side. "A documentary."

"About women and what you all have to go through every day. How scared you are all the time, just to have a man walking behind you on the sidewalk. I wanted to get a real reaction." He presses his hands together as contritely as he can. "I see now that was the wrong way to go about it."

"Oh I see," She-Ra says with exaggerated mock forgiveness. "Well that makes everything better. Were you filming a documentary last Halloween when you followed me? Or what about Heather over there? Were you making a movie when you scared her half to death on Saint Patrick's Day? Or Kiana on the Fourth of July?"

Todd has never known their names. He prefers to follow women to whom he is anonymous, just in case they get a good look at him. Hearing their names makes him flinch as if he's been struck.

Through the headset draped around his neck, Jonah's voice comes softly. "We're on our way, Todd. Get out of there if you can." And then the rustle of Jonah removing his own headset.

"I have a camera," Todd says, straightening his back, trying to look defiant. He taps his collar where the tiny camera is clipped. "Your face is already recorded for posterity. All of you." He shines the phone around again, trying to illuminate the girls surrounding him, who wince away from the bright light. When he gets to Cat Girl, she chitters and his sweaty hand drops the phone to the ground with a clatter.

Todd lunges to pick up the phone again. Cat Girl leaps into his way. At least he can't see her face, he thinks, backing away from her and into another of the girls. They've surrounded him and the monster, and when he tries to dart through the spaces between them, the girls hit him with bats and crowbars and a two-by-four with a nail in it, to judge by how their weapons feel against his arms and legs.

They're trying to keep him in the circle. With Cat Girl. With a monster.

He falls to his knees in front of She-Ra, bruised and aching. He just needs to buy time. "Please, let me go, and I'll never follow anyone ever again. I'm so sorry. I see how wrong I was."

She-Ra shakes her head, dimly visible in the light still shining up from the dropped phone. "Nah, sorry. We'll have to pass. Do you have any idea how much trouble it was to summon her?" She gestures toward Cat Girl, who hovers just behind him, shifting her weight and warbling. "Expensive, too. She came all this way, and it can't be for nothing."

"All this just for following you home? You're psycho."

She rolls her eyes. "Negging isn't going to work, either, bruh. Look, we all know that eventually following girls home was going to lose its appeal. And when that happened, you were going to start doing way more harmful stuff to get your rocks off. This is how serial killers get started."

"My friends will come for me," he blurts.

She grins, raising the crowbar and nodding to the creature behind him. "We're counting on it."

Cat Girl gibbers and dives for him. Todd screams and screams, the sound echoing off the empty, half-finished houses.

# A GRACE OF FINER FORM

We worried first about the polar bears, my mother told me, but nobody cared much about polar bears. Next, we worried about the bees, which was much more pressing, for reasons I didn't completely understand. And then, of course, finally, as the ice caps melted and the seas rose and the freshwater lakes dried up, we worried about ourselves. I asked her so many times how it was that people didn't see the end coming, when they were warned for so many years, but my mother would shrug and look away, in those days, when she would still talk about it.

Later, I understood the guilt and shame that must have pressed on her and driven her to silence, and, eventually, to a dark place where she took her own life. I was so accustomed to her coldness and distance that her death barely registered. I was alone for the first time in my life, but I'd always been lonely, so it wasn't as great a change as you might expect. I buried my mother down the hill from the spring, where her body could nurture the trees. Out of the hardest wood I could find, I carved for her a marker in the rough image of the naiad who blessed our spring, whispering to myself the stories of gods and titans she had told me so many nights around our fire.

I stayed at the spring where we had lived for so many years, the water a dangerous life-giving secret. I kept the same routines. Everything I did was for one purpose: to keep myself alive. My mother had, after all, clung to life for nearly twenty years in order to teach me how, abandoning the comforts of civilization for my benefit. Living was the only thing I could do to honor her memory.

There was little joy in it. My mother had taught me few of life's pleasures. I knew a few songs, though, and at night I raised my voice to the trees. Sometimes the creatures that lived in the forest sang with me, a harmonious echo of howls and chirps. Over many seasons, some of the animals grew closer to the spring, daring to drink the water while I watched from nearby. My mother's admonitions reverberated in my head when a six-legged doe, fat with the promise of fawns, nested in the thicket near my cave. Mother would have frightened her away, but I let her stay. It was better than being alone.

I had never understood mother's fear of the mutated forest creatures. She, of course, had remembered a time when the animals weren't the distorted versions we had now, with extra limbs, and eyes in the wrong places, and wings or tails that didn't belong. But, to me, the two-headed chipmunk-lizard hybrid that scrambled up my sleeve one afternoon to take a seed from my hand was as natural as any other thing in the forest. These twisted animals were all I had ever known.

Sometimes, at night, while I lay lonely on my lumpy cot, shivering beside the dying embers of my fire, I thought I heard the whisper of leaves and crack of branches, like something massive moving through the forest. But when I rose to investigate, there was no sign of anything. I began to wonder if I was losing my mind. Maybe I was just as warped as the other denizens of the forest, but my unnaturalness took a different form.

Two humans arrived one winter morning while I bathed in the hot springs. They were so covered in clothes—utility trousers and heavy jackets and handkerchiefs and hats—I couldn't even tell whether they were human. Every story my mother had instilled in me about men and the other dangerous creatures in the world raced through my mind, a jumble of terror. I imagined the chipmunk-lizard hybrid and what horrors would result from similar human distortions. Every cell in my body screamed that I should grab my gun to defend myself and my water. Instead, naked and vulnerable, I was paralyzed.

"Is that a hot spring?" One of them exclaimed, her voice high like my mother's.

The other removed her pack and pulled the bandana from her face. She was a woman. Her cheeks were red and her lips chapped, but her eyes were bright and silently begging a question. When I made no indication either way, she fearlessly stripped off all her supplies and clothing and lowered herself into the steaming water. The other woman did the same.

Fear coursed through me, my own blood pounding in my ears. My mother's disembodied voice scolded me for allowing them so close.

But they were filthy, exhausted, injured. Their ribs showed through their skin. One was covered in livid purple bruises and the other had a long gash down her arm bandaged with a dirty rag. Filth sloughed from their bodies, turning the spring water briefly gray, until both women were pink as baby mice. They were harmless.

No one is harmless, my mother's voice assured me. I thought of the chipmunk-lizard and the doe. None of the forest's creatures had ever harmed me. These women didn't seem very different. Mother had filled my ears with warnings about men and their depravity, but had never mentioned women and what dangers they might impose.

They introduced themselves to me as Amber and Kelly. When I asked how they had found my spring, Amber said they'd heard me singing at night and followed the sound of my song. Kelly called my voice beautiful, angelic, a beacon of hope in the darkness. No one had ever complimented me before. My heart felt as if it would swell too big for my chest.

I would do anything to hang onto the feeling those compliments inspired. Was it joy? Bliss? I had never felt something so divine.

I told them they could stay. There were plenty of resources for three, as long as they were willing to work, and as long as they swore to defend the spring as ruthlessly as my mother had taught me. They agreed to these terms.

I taught them how to properly care for a wound, how to start and tend a fire, how to clean and use the guns in my cache, how to tend the spring, how to make offerings to the naiad, and how to dry herbs and preserve plants so we could feed ourselves over the winter. Our lives settled into a pleasant rhythm. I was shocked by how ignorant they were in the necessary tasks for survival. They were like children, at first, and I found myself channeling my mother's patient instructions as I taught them how to do everything, even simple tasks like digging a latrine pit far from the cave or boiling spring water so it would be safe to drink.

To their credit, both women learned quickly and neither shirked her responsibilities. With three to share the daily tasks, there was more time for joy, and while I taught Amber and Kelly to survive, they taught me to really live. We bathed together, slept together, gathered wood together, and performed the ritual offerings together. At night, we raised our voices to the stars together. For the first time in my life, I was happy.

Yes, sometimes I missed my solitude. Kelly talked too much —especially about men, an obsession I couldn't begin to understand—and Amber's laugh sometimes made my skin prickle. They complained about my aversion to killing animals that made us all vegetarians. They both acted as if the offerings to the naiad were silly, and rolled their eyes when I retold them the mythical tales of gods and heroes I had learned from my mother.

But it was still better than being alone. Sometimes, in the night, I still heard the rustling of leaves and snapping of branches that made me imagine something taller than any tree walking through the forest. I would nestle in closer to my friends and match my breathing to theirs until I returned to sleep.

Amber and Kelly told me stories about the world outside the forest. About how, while my mother took me into the trees and made a life for us around the spring, the rest of the world had tried to go on. Their families continued to send them to school even as water rations dwindled. The powerful hoarded the best of everything, leaving the dregs for everyone else. There were riots over food. Life in the cities became unbearable as the temperatures rose and electricity became less reliable. Heat stroke became a common way to die in the summer, while starvation and hypothermia took lives in the winter. It didn't all happen at once, the destruction of society. It happened in fits and starts, slowly, over many years, before things were so bad it was clear nothing was working like it should, and it was impossible to continue living in the city.

Their families tried to move to the country, but the countryside was already swarming with desperate people and dangerously mutated animals. I held my rifle close and was grateful for the lessons my mother had taught me. And I was grateful that my mother had taken her own life, instead of wasting away of thirst, being attacked by one of the deformed predators that lived in the forest, dying a long, lingering death from infection, or getting shot by other desperate water-seekers. Amber and Kelly made a long, tragic list of their dead. I had not known, before then, there were so many ways to die.

There were stories, they said, of a haven in the north, a place where water flowed freely and people lived in harmony. They were going there when they stumbled upon my singing. Their water rations were dangerously low, and the creatures that lurked in the forest had started coming too close. Finding me had likely saved their lives. They were so grateful.

I told them I was grateful for their company. I hadn't known how unhappy I was before they came. I confessed that it seemed like the fates had brought us together, to care for each other and be a family, forever.

They looked at each other awkwardly. Amber licked her lips. Kelly cleared her throat.

They were leaving, I knew then. They didn't have to say it. Hadn't we spent weeks together, months, the whole of winter? Didn't I know the meaning of every twitch and glare? They were still planning to go to this fabled haven, this imaginary place of endless freshwater and harmonious living. The naiad's spring and I were only a temporary way station. Now that their bodies were healthy and their canteens filled, they would be on the road again, as soon as it was clear of snow.

My heart felt like it was made of sharp glass, stabbing my chest every time I breathed.

"Come with us," Amber said. "You can't stay here forever. What kind of life would that be?"

If only they would stay, it would be a joyful life, I thought. A content life. No men, but few problems. All the water they could drink. All the companionship they could ever need. I gazed at my mother's grave down the hillside and set my jaw.

That night, the earth trembled beneath me while I slept, and I dreamed of many arms holding me while I sobbed. The next morning the snow had melted. Amber and Kelly were gone, and the forest was silent, as if all the birds that chirped and insects that clicked had gone silent in deference to my grief.

I didn't know true sorrow when my mother died, but she had not held me skin-to-skin on the cold, dark nights while dogs howled outside our drafty home. She had not taught me songs about love, had not told me jokes from the world before, had not bathed with me in the spring and playfully splashed me. She had not made me laugh. She had not brought me joy.

But Amber and Kelly had, so now I knew sorrow, down to my bones. I knew the miserable keening of loss, because it forced its way from my throat. Grief burrowed its way into my chest, into my soul, and a dark veil was pulled across the world. The sky was the color of ash, and food tasted like dirt.

I tried to keep my routine. I tried to go through the motions, doing the things my mother had taught me to do, to preserve my life. But without Kelly and Amber, without love, I could see little reason to stay alive. Loneliness was worse, now that I had known its opposite.

All I wanted to do was sleep the day away, and that would lead to my death. The perimeter had to be maintained, the spring protected. Food had to be gathered and stored, water collected and boiled, offerings made to the naiad. There was too much to do to wallow, but I didn't want to do any of it.

As the first crocuses poked their heads from the frost-rimed earth, I gathered supplies, loaded my guns, and went north.

That first day, I walked the road alone. Eventually I came upon a recently-abandoned campsite. I didn't know to whom it belonged, but I piled wood on the embers and camped there, imagining that Amber and Kelly were just ahead, and I slept where they had slept.

I went on like this for days, moving north unerringly, following the long black snake of the road that disappeared on the horizon. My legs ached and my feet burned, my boots giving them new and exciting blisters. I lay awake in the darkness each night, terrified to be so far from my home, my feet throbbing and bleeding. I wanted to turn back so many times, but I didn't know if I could find my way back to the spring. My water rations ran low.

I encountered no one, not even the usual wild animals with their assortments of mismatched eyes, and the loneliness became oppressive. Out here, I couldn't even hear the voice of my mother. Death was close behind me. If I died so far from the spring, what would happen to my spirit? Would I wander the road alone eternally? This thought kept me going past the point of reason, limping northward long after I should have made myself rest and let myself heal.

On the distant horizon, something moved against the clouds. It was dusk, and my vision had never been good, so the image was hazy. It looked like an enormous person, tall as a mountain. Was I hallucinating? Was this what people saw before they died?

Laughter, as familiar to me as my own, rose up from the trees ahead, and I dried my face and managed to mince up to the campsite. The laughter faded when I stepped into the firelight. Amber and Kelly were there, but they looked different. Kelly's eyes were too shiny, and Amber's mouth was strangely slack. They held bottles of brown liquid in their hands and waved them about, crying my name and running to embrace me. I should have felt relieved, or excited, but I felt only dread when I saw their companions.

Men. They were just as my mother had described them: taller than women, broader across the shoulders, great hulking versions of us with square jaws and hair on their faces. They stank like wild animals and they radiated menace.

I begged for Amber and Kelly to come home with me. They couldn't see it, but these men were making them strange and wrong. They laughed and shooed me away. The men stood in threatening poses until I staggered away into the brush to make my own camp nearby.

All night I eavesdropped on their conversation. "We have to go before dawn. We don't want her following us," Amber half-whispered, her speech slurred.

A man's gruff voice: "I thought she shared her food with you and stitched you up and all that. Why are you so scared of her?"

"She's a nice enough kid. But...you ever have someone get way too attached to you? Like stalker-level attached?"

The man chortled. "Sure. She's harmless though."

"Nah," Kelly said. "I know her type. She seems harmless, but you gotta be careful. We should sleep in shifts, watching out. Otherwise she might shiv us in our sleep."

That prompted laughter from the group. I clapped my hands over my ears but I could still hear Amber's voice, cutting through the darkness like a knife.

"It's not like that. She just thought there was more between us than there was. We wanted to go north to find a haven and she was never going to leave her spring. So we just left. It was best for everyone, she just didn't know it. I can't believe she came after us! So stupid."

Her words burned like a wasp sting, pulsing in my chest, an open wound. I had mistakenly thought Amber and Kelly loved me as I loved them, but they'd brushed me away the moment they saw me. I had bandaged their wounds and fed them and kept them safe, and here I was with bleeding feet and empty canteens, going to sleep on the cold, wet forest floor only fifty feet from their campsite while they cavorted with men who had given them nothing but liquor. I wondered if I could find my way home to the spring before I died of dehydration. I held back my tears, mindful of wasting water on emotion.

In the morning, the massive thing on the horizon was closer, resolving itself into a towering titan's form, still hazy in the dawn light. It was a person, but with too many limbs, too many faces, pearlescent skin shimmering in the sunlight, horrible and wonderful to behold. It was so tall its faces were wreathed in clouds like a crown. Around the titan's head, winged creatures wheeled and dipped like a god's heralds. At its feet, a retinue followed, at this distance appearing like a seething mass.

This mountainous person wasn't a hallucination at all. I had to warn my friends. I limped to their campsite and it was abandoned, the remnants of the fire ring still smoking. I ran to the road barefoot, no longer able to pull my boots over my swollen feet, leaving behind me a trail of blood.

Amber and Kelly and their men were on the road, fully clothed and burdened with packs, but they were walking south.

I screamed at them. "Where are you going? Your mythical haven is to the north."

The men laughed with that same dismissive chortle. Amber and Kelly at least had the good sense to look ashamed. One of the men said, "Why go to the north when there's a spring and a cave a few days' walk to the south?"

When my heart broke, I swear it made a sound like stone cracking in two. I collapsed to my knees. The ground shook beneath me as if an earthquake were about to tear the earth apart, and I turned to find the titan moving toward us with great strides that ate the miles in moments. Its faces turned and turned so that each pair of eyes could behold me there, on the ground, the naiad too far from her spring, the trail of blood behind me. It stood over me, five-breasted and seven-armed, three phalluses dangling between its many legs. What I had taken for a pearlescent shimmer at a distance was actually the oscillation of the vegetation that sprouted from the titan's skin, long-stemmed mushrooms and coiling vines and bell-shaped flowers the size of a dog waving and juddering with each of the giant's steps. The creatures swarming the air, flying joyful loops around the titan's body, were the hybrid monsters I was used to seeing, only moreso: the wings of an eagle combined with the body of a lynx, but also the eyes of an insect, the paws of a raccoon, the tail of a snake. Horrifying and miraculous all at once.

Water sluiced from the titan's skin and over me like a torrential rainstorm, like a refreshing summer downpour. I swallowed what I could, letting the rest drench me down to my bones, knowing it would change me and longing for that change.

Hands lifted me up and they were the hands of the titan's worshippers, men and women who had once been human. They were so much more, now, with ten arms and twenty legs and countless faces. They were furred and feathered and scaled. They regarded me with yellow eyes with slitted pupils or the unnerving square pupils of a goat. When they kissed me, their lips tasted of nectar.

The titan's tears healed my injuries, those of the flesh and those of my spirit, until I felt as if I would burst into sunbeams. I had thought I knew true happiness in companionship, but it was nothing close to this divine feeling of completeness. I would never know loneliness again, and I wanted all of humanity to know this enlightenment.

The men fired weapons at the titan, ammunition from guns stolen from my cache. The titan ignored the bullets the way a man would ignore a mosquito. The mass of worshippers fell on them, ravening, filling the air with the scent of blood.

Amber and Kelly ran, screaming. I followed them, pursuing them doggedly into the trees. I was faster, now, the titan's tears making me an ideal version of myself, one that felt no pain, one that had no hesitation. I enclosed them in my embrace, my arms lengthening and my flesh stretching to encompass them wholly in the love of a goddess. They shrieked and struggled but I knew what was best for us. I knew how I could keep them safe and happy forever.

And we would never be alone again.

The titan's tears melted their skin and melded it with mine. Our bones snapped together into one skeleton, our hair braided itself into one wild tangle. Amber and Kelly and I became one creature with six legs and six arms and three faces, weeping with terrible joy. The warped creatures in the titan's parade caressed us with welcoming hands, cooed over our raw beauty, whispered appreciation for our sacrifice.

My mother told me the titans created man in their image. And now, with the seas risen and the lake beds dry, they had returned to remake us in their image once again.

We turned north and began to walk.

# CHORUS OF WHISPERS

Orphelia's procedure took place on a sunny Monday afternoon. She and her mother arrived early and stood in line outside the surgery with other mothers and daughters, waiting their turn, the temperature gradually rising until Orphelia's clothes grew scratchy and hot, and her skin tender to the touch.

Eventually they made it into the shade of the waiting room. Orphelia's stomach growled but she didn't complain about her hunger; Mummy had already told her she wasn't allowed to eat before the procedure. She watched as other girls her age were dragged from the surgical suite by weeping mothers. Some of the girls walked stiff-legged, with wide eyes and ashen faces. Others clutched at their mothers and wept soundlessly.

Orphelia's legs quivered and she wanted to run from the room. Her mother's huge, sweaty hand gripped her tiny one. When it was her turn, Orphelia's mother signed various papers and the nurse stamped them. Mummy folded up and tucked them into the pocket of her voluminous skirt.

They went into the surgical suite. There was a tall doctor in a white coat, a big chair with straps on the arms. An injection made the world go fuzzy and gray. When she roused, moments later, her throat was on fire. She wanted to scream but air passing over her savaged larynx was agony. The pain was so severe the world tilted sideways when she tried to sit up. Mummy offered her a hand and Orphelia slid obediently from the chair. Her legs wobbled under her and Mummy gave her a moment to get them under herself before gently guiding her from the surgical suite.

The girls standing in the waiting room stared at her, looking for some sign of what was in store for them. Orphelia wanted to warn them. She wanted to tell them it was horrible, the worst pain you could possibly imagine. She wanted to tell them to run. When she took a breath deep enough to speak, a thousand needles stabbed her throat, and she could only gasp and fall forward into Mummy's waiting arms. She was carried home, weeping silent tears of pain and betrayal.

This would be Orphelia's first memory.

Orphelia used her brother's workshop at night, while the family slept, tinkering and testing, researching and revising. The blueprints spread on the workbench looked like the scrawlings of a madwoman, her brother said, but she had not had the benefit of his formal engineer's training. She had only the limited numbers and letters she had learned in school and the small amount of secret training her father and brother had allowed her. It was forbidden to teach girls complex math, physics, or medicine. Still, Orphelia devoured books from the family library when no one was looking. She did her best to absorb them, looking up words in dictionaries and thesauruses, reading every footnote and carefully inspecting and recreating every diagram until she had the best understanding she could manage.

She knew her project was probably futile, especially if anyone were to catch her. But, like many great inventors, she was motivated by spite: every time a prototype failed or research led to a dead end, she would remember the afternoon of her procedure and would try again.

Tonight, she crouched over the workbench, attempting to affix a length of jellyfish tentacle to the inside of a narrow copper ring, using a glue she'd made herself by boiling hooves she'd bought from a butcher. She wore only her bloomers and a camisole, sensitive to the heat of the workshop—or any heat at all—ever since that Monday afternoon. Her hair was swept into a messy chignon and her feet slid around inside her brother's too-big work boots. She'd stuffed the toes with rags and started wearing them after she'd ruined a pair of silk slippers during one of her experiments, which had earned her a thrashing.

A soft touch on her shoulder made her jump. Her mother stood there, lips pressed together, regretful expression on her face. *Sorry,* she mouthed.

Orphelia's mother was one of the few unfortunate women upon whom the procedure was completely effective. She hadn't been able to say a single word without extreme pain since she was three years old. Of course, breathing was also agony, and she rarely slept as a result, but the medical establishment considered the procedure a total success. Maude was an ideal case written about in textbooks.

*I'm busy, Mum. What do you need?* Orphelia whispered. She was lucky not to have lingering pain after the wounds of the procedure had healed, and she still had a voice—only a whisper, but better than nothing. From her perspective, anyway. Many people felt differently, especially because she wasn't afraid to use what little voice she still possessed.

*Have you thought about Dr. Carver's offer?* Maude smiled hopefully.

Orphelia's shoulders slumped.

Maude's smile faded. *He expects an answer by tomorrow morning.*

*I know.*

Maude's hand went to her daughter's arm. *Your father and I were very lucky to marry for love. That's rare. You may not love Dr. Carver, but he can make you comfortable. Papa and I won't be around forever to take care of you.*

Orphelia shrugged and bent over the jellyfish tentacles again. *Quincy and I will look after each other.*

Maude made a scoffing sound that must have hurt and threw up her arms in frustration. She didn't bother to make the rest of the argument. They'd had this talk so many times, Orphelia could play the rest of it in her head. Maude would say that Quincy would want to get married eventually, and what wife would want a man saddled with a spinster sister? Orphelia would reply that Quincy didn't care about getting married and would rather live a quiet life in the countryside with his sister in a house so big they only had to see each other at suppertime. She would add that she was focused on her project, and no husband would let her complete it. A husband would expect her to manage a household and care for children, neither of which held any interest for Orphelia.

And Maude would point out Orphelia's age, which would make her a humiliating failure if she didn't accept an offer soon. Dr. Carver was a good man, and Orphelia would admit that if she were to consider any offer seriously, it would be his, but she simply had no interest in marriage and would not be forced into it.

Maude scowled. For the first time, she mouthed, *This project is ruining your life, O. I should burn it all.* Quick as a snake, she shot across the room and ripped the blueprints off the wall in one swift motion.

Orphelia made a choked sound, the closest thing she could manage to a scream. She ran to Maude and they wrestled over the designs, the paper tearing and crumpling. Orphelia wept and wheezed. Her mother's face was red as she marched from the workshop with her hands full of torn blueprints. Croaking desperately, Orphelia followed her mother into the kitchen and managed one bark of rage as Maude tossed the papers into the smoldering fire in the hearth.

Maude turned to her daughter with fury in her eyes. *You will accept Dr. Carver. I'll send the note in the morning.* She turned and swept upstairs to her own bedroom, and the discussion was ended.

Orphelia knelt in front of the hearth, watching the bits of paper burn. Her mother had never, ever treated her this way before. Of course, Orphelia had never been twenty-seven before. She would already be the oldest bride in the newspaper announcements. And Papa's health had not been good of late. Maude was worried about what would happen to the family if Papa didn't survive his next bout of pancreatitis. Quincy had a brilliant mind for engineering, but was not a great businessman, and would struggle to care for both his sister and mother as the head of family.

Maude wanted the best for her daughter, Orphelia knew. But huge tears still slid down her cheeks as she watched the work of years go up in flames. She clenched her jaw in determination and went upstairs, where she dressed in several layers, packed a few things into a case, and took what money she had squirrelled away. She went to the workshop and packed up a few tools, supplies, and the most useful books into the smallest lockbox she could find. She crammed even more into the pockets of her skirts, vest, and jacket.

She didn't know what destination she had in mind as she pulled her black wool cape over her shoulders and swept from the family home. She just knew she couldn't stay here.

~

Orphelia made her way into the heart of town. She had considered calling on cousins or family friends or even school acquaintances to put her up, but had rejected those options, because any of those people would report her whereabouts to her parents. So, she made her way from the posh part of town to the merchant class neighborhoods, where a few people still wandered late at night, mostly stumbling drunks. The flickering streetlamps cast faint, greasy light onto uneven cobbles as Orphelia staggered along in heeled boots. The air smelled like burning oil and raw sewage. The atmosphere made her skin prickle, and every shadow made her gut roil. She carried her mother's warnings about being a woman out in the world alone, and her father's recitation each morning of the murders that had happened overnight while the family slept safely in their beds, dutifully reported in the newspaper. To be out after dark was tempting fate.

Orphelia's heart raced and she almost went home. No one would have to know she'd left. Tomorrow, Maude would send a note to Dr. Carver; he would visit, and a date would be set for her wedding. Soon enough, she would have children of her own. She would have daughters, and when they were three years old, she would march them to the surgery for the procedure.

She pressed on, into the darkness.

As she passed an alley, there was a sound, as of someone being punched and the air gusting from their lungs. Orphelia sucked in a breath and turned to look involuntarily. The darkness writhed with undefined shapes. A second *whuff* convinced her someone was, in fact, being attacked. There! Scuffling and the clicking of heeled boots on the cobbles. She knew she should turn away and flee, but what if a woman was being attacked? A woman who couldn't cry out because the procedure had taken that privilege from her.

Orphelia glanced down the street, hoping for a uniformed officer or a brave-looking gentleman, but saw no one. With a deep inhale for courage, she dropped her case and lockbox into the shadows behind a trash bin. Drawing herself up to her full height, she strode into the alley. She nearly tripped over a piece of wood, which she lifted in her hands as a weapon.

As she approached, the picture became clearer. Several

women in black dresses crouched over a prone form. One of them carried a lantern turned down as low as the flame would allow. As they reeled back from the body, one of them cradling something against her stomach, Orphelia saw a man. His eyes were open and staring, his mouth slack-jawed, and his throat torn away, a bloody wreck.

Orphelia had seen corpses before, when her brother snuck her into the anatomy laboratory at his university, but those had been skinned, muscle on display, organs removed, faces covered, flesh cold. This man was still warm. One of his legs kicked and his chest quivered as if he still tried to draw breath.

Orphelia dropped the piece of wood to the cobbles with a clatter. Her gloved hands flew to cover her mouth and she gasped, tears springing to her eyes.

As one, the women turned to her. They were young, younger than she was expecting, with faces ranging from pale to dark, and expressions ranging from panicked to resolute.

*Hypatia,* one of them hissed to the girl holding the bloody thing. She presented Hypatia with a box and the other girl slipped it inside.

Hypatia turned her attention to Orphelia. With a movement like a scorpion extending its tail, she flicked out a razor, the sort a barber might use to shave a gentleman's beard. Orphelia wanted to run but her legs refused to work. Instead, she whispered *What are you doing? What is this?*

*None of your business,* Hypatia hissed. *Can you forget what happened here?*

A chorus of rasping voices:

*Look at her.*

*This is the most exciting thing she's ever seen.*

*She'll never forget.*

*And she heard your name.*

*You know what we do to witnesses. Even women.*

Orphelia's legs finally worked and she turned to run, but her boots caught in her long cape and the fabric twisted around her ankles. She hit the ground hard, skinning her palms against the rough cobblestones.

The girls were on her like hunting dogs on a fox. Feet kicked her ribs and Orphelia curled into a ball to protect her organs. Fists punched at her arms, shoulder, face and chest. Someone's boot stomped at her face and she rolled away with a screech of terror that came out as a squeak, no louder than the sound made by a mouse.

Hypatia pulled her hair, yanking Orphelia's head back. The razor was cold against the flesh of her throat.

*Wait!* One girl's whisper was almost normal volume. *Hypatia, wait!*

*What?*

*Look at this! It fell out of her pocket.*

Orphelia, trembling with her murderer's blade at her neck, wondered what they could possibly have found. She didn't remember what she had crammed into her pockets. Springs, screwdrivers, books, curls of fine-gauge wire, a vial of jellyfish tentacles. What could possibly interest this gang of murderesses?

The razor fell away and the pressure on her hair increased. Orphelia scrambled up to a sitting position.

Hypatia thrust a book into her face. *Is this yours?*

Orphelia squinted at it. She didn't know. She couldn't see the words on the cover.

Someone turned up the flame in the oil lamp and brought it closer. The book was *Buchanan's Manual of Anatomy.* Orphelia nodded, her eyes finding Hypatia's in the lamplight. The girl's irises were nearly as pale as her face. She looked about fifteen or sixteen years old, with bright flaxen hair. She would have been pretty, if not for a long, ragged scar down one cheek.

*What do you know of anatomy?* Hypatia asked, breath reeking of stale beer.

Orphelia could only guess why she inquired. The girls looked dirty and bedraggled up close, and they stank of unwashed bodies. Perhaps they were seeking a doctor for their various injuries?

*I know it by heart,* Orphelia admitted.

*Could you do surgery?* Hypatia hissed.

Orphelia nodded, grateful the girl asked if she *could* and not if she ever *had.* The answers to those two questions were very different.

In a dingy attic room in Madame Pepper's Boardinghouse, the girls arrayed themselves around the room, removing boots and jackets, unlacing corsets, and generally making themselves comfortable. The room was the length of Madame Pepper's entire house. Several mattresses were unrolled on the floor, and various mismatched chests, small tables, and a single dresser missing all its drawers filled the space.

The lamp was turned up to full illumination. The girls cleared the chairs and eating implements from a small table and Hypatia jumped up onto it, seating herself with ankles crossed casually. She presented the lockbox to Orphelia.

Orphelia opened the box gingerly, not sure what to expect. The box was filled to the brim with rapidly melting ice. On top of the ice was a bloody, fleshy lump. Orphelia pulled a pencil from her skirt pocket and prodded it carefully. There was skin, and connective tissue, in the shape of a tube. It was the man's throat, which Hypatia had cut raggedly from his neck, including his larynx.

She suddenly understood what Hypatia was asking. *It can't be done.*

Rage flared in Hypatia's pale eyes and the razor flashed in her hand. *Are you saying you can't, or won't?*

*It's impossible.*

*Why?*

*The larynx is tangled up with the thyroid gland. It's almost impossible to separate the two.*

*So?*

*To remove your larynx and replace it with this one...it would almost certainly kill your thyroid. And you need your thyroid to live.*

Hypatia sucked in a breath and her mouth puckered. *How long could I live without one?*

Orphelia recoiled. *No one knows, exactly. It's a mystery what compounds your thyroid releases into your bloodstream.*

The girl raised her chin. *Do it, then.*

*Here?*

Hypatia nodded.

*I can't. This place is filthy. I don't have medical tools, or anesthesia...*

*We have those things,* another girl rasped.

*Venus is a nurse,* Hypatia whispered. *She can assist you.* Her hand went to her throat, massaging it, as if even this small amount of speech caused her pain.

Orphelia steeled herself, shaking her head. *I can't. It's much too dangerous. You'll die.*

The razor flashed to her throat. The girls surrounded her, their bodies pressing uncomfortably close. *No, she won't,* Venus hissed. *What happens to her, happens to you.*

Orphelia weighed her options. She could confess to her lack of medical experience right now. But if she did, these crazed girls wouldn't hesitate to throw her from the roof of Madame Pepper's Boardinghouse. Performing the surgery was the best choice she had. At least there was a chance Hypatia might survive, and thus Orphelia might as well.

She sighed, the exhalation scraping past her own mangled vocal cords. She raised her chin, removed her cape with a flourish, and accepted the box of excised human flesh.

~

Orphelia tried to perform the surgery quickly. Breathing through a tube could not be comfortable, even with anesthesia, and she feared Hypatia waking while she was still removing the remains of her larynx or inserting the new one. Her hands shook as she stitched the new larynx in place. The organ was too large for the girl's slim neck, and it would probably bulge and cause her pain forever.

At least she could be proud of how she managed to preserve Hypatia's thyroid, coiled around the front of her neck like a fat snake, protecting her throat. If they could keep her from getting an infection, she might actually survive this reverse procedure.

When she finished stitching Hypatia's throat closed, Orphelia collapsed into a puddle on the floor.

*She lives, for now.* Venus announced authoritatively in the heavy silence, her voice nearly as loud as a man's softest speech, her fingers pressing into Hypatia's wrist. The other girls turned wide eyes full of wonder to the surgeon weeping on the floor.

There was still so much that could go wrong, but Orphelia didn't point this out. She let the girls undress her, pull a clean nightgown over her head, and guide her onto one of the stinking mattresses. She fell asleep staring at a mouse hole in the wall.

She woke sometime later to someone plying her with warm, salty broth. She gulped it down without opening her eyes more than a crack, and then went back to sleep again. Exhaustion was like a heavy weight around her ankles, pulling her underwater.

When she woke again, it was to the sound of excited chatter. One of the girls crouched beside Orphelia's mattress. *You awake?* The girl mouthed.

Orphelia nodded and pulled herself to a sitting position. Her limbs were heavy as stones and her stomach growled. Her mouth tasted like she'd been eating roadkill. *How long have I been asleep?*

The girl held up three fingers.

Orphelia started and scrambled to her feet, casting about the dark room. *How is Hypatia?* Girls and women dressed in black crowded the attic space.

The girl offered her a black blouse, skirt, and waist cinch much like the ones she wore.

*No, thank you. I'd rather wear my clothes.*

*Sold,* the girl mouthed. She tapped her chest and mouthed, *Winifred.*

*Sold?* Anger and fear lanced through Orphelia's chest. *You sold my things?*

Winifred shook her head. *Not me.*

Venus appeared from the crowd. *Your things were sold to benefit the revolution. These clothes should fit, Doctor Waverly.*

Orphelia started again. She wanted to ask how they knew her surname, but then she thought about her travel case embossed with her initials, the velvet jacket with her first name embroidered on the breast, and the delicate lace waves sewn to the hem of her cape. It wouldn't take too much work to put those pieces together if you were clever.

*I'm not a doctor,* Orphelia protested.

*You are now.* Venus offered Orphelia a slim pamphlet printed on ivory paper.

*Dr. Orphelia Waverly has performed the greatest miracle: returning human speech to the female throat!* The pamphlet proclaimed. *See the wonder in the flesh when Hypatia Crane-Hemsby SPEAKS at sunset on April 26th on the steps of City Hall.* Beneath this, in a flowing, cursive script, was written: *Government Men and Church Elders, we recommend you cease and desist robbing girls and women of their voices, or WE WILL TAKE YOURS.*

There were two women sketched in the middle of the pamphlet, with remarkably good likenesses: Orphelia and Hypatia. Orphelia's stomach dropped and her skin went suddenly clammy.

*You've ruined me,* she gasped.

Venus clapped a strong hand on Orphelia's arm. *No, friend. We've made you the key to the revolution.*

Orphelia folded herself back onto the mattress, staring at the pamphlet. Winifred quietly placed the clothes beside her. The two women turned to join the others, who were making their way downstairs.

*Wait,* Orphelia called after them, her loudest call a harsh croak.

Venus turned back.

*April 26th would be in only...* her muddled brain tried to do the math, but she couldn't remember what date it had been when she fled her family home.

*Three days,* Venus said.

*Will Hypatia be able to speak by then? That's so soon. The swelling...*

Venus stared down her nose at Orphelia. *She heals quickly. She'll be fine.* And then Venus made her way to the ladder and down, leaving Orphelia alone in the suddenly drafty attic in only a nightgown.

Orphelia dressed quickly. The blouse was tight, and the black skirt and petticoat were much too long and would require hemming. The only item in her possession unsold by the revolutionaries were her boots, which were a dark enough green to appear black, especially under these too-long skirts. Winifred had left her a black ribbon to tie up her hair, as the other girls did, but Orphelia drew the line there. She raked her fingers through her tousled mane and hoped some few of her curls still remained. Without a mirror, it was difficult to tell. She imagined she must look frightful and couldn't help thinking what her mother would say. She could almost see Maude's lips mouthing, *You really must make more of an effort, O.*

Tears rose to her eyes at the thought of her mother. She dashed them away. Her stomach rumbled again and she moved to the ladder, throwing her legs over so she could climb down.

Rough hands caught her and pushed her back up into the attic. *What are you doing?* She demanded when she regained her breath, staring down the ladder at two black-clad women. One was small and wiry, and the other was tall and stocky, like a farmgirl from a provincial tale.

The small one shook her head slowly and pointed to the attic. The communication was clear enough: Orphelia was to remain upstairs.

*I'm hungry,* Orphelia complained, pressing her hand to her stomach.

The small one nodded at her companion. The larger woman moved in front of the ladder and stared up at the captive while the smaller one slipped out of view, hopefully in search of sustenance.

With a sigh, Orphelia settled her skirts around her like a nest and waited.

~

Hypatia appeared the following afternoon with a group of new recruits. A black scarf was tied around her throat. She sat beside Orphelia on her mattress and handed her a pasty wrapped in paper, still warm.

*You sold my things,* Orphelia whispered.

*Not the important things.* Smirking, Hypatia rose and went to the drawerless dresser, pulling out some clothes and dumping them on the floor so she could reach deep inside and remove Orphelia's lockbox.

Orphelia snatched it from her hands and opened it eagerly, fingers gliding across the implements and prototypes, unpacking each with tender care. Tears of overwhelming relief stung her eyes.

*You should let me see your throat,* Orphelia whispered, closing the lockbox and hiding it under her skirts as she reseated herself on the mattress. She unwrapped the pasty and tucked in gratefully.

*Venus is caring for me.* Hypatia's words were barely a whisper, inaudible over the crinkling of the paper pasty wrapper. Fortunately, Orphelia had a lot of experience reading lips.

*Is Venus a nurse the way I'm a doctor?*

Hypatia shrugged and frowned. She didn't look Orphelia in the eyes as she untied the scarf and let it fall away. Hypatia's face was pale, but her neck was red and splotchy with purple bruising that was visible even in the dim light streaming in the filthy attic window. Her neck was swollen and lumpy, straining Orphelia's neat stitches.

Orphelia shook her head. *You should be in bed. You need to rest.*

*I feel fine.*

*You don't look fine.*

*I'm recovering very well.*

*You could die!*

Hypatia turned to Orphelia, settling those eerie, near-translucent eyes on her. *We're all going to die. When I'm gone,* she paused to wince and her fingers came to her throat, hovering as if she wished she could touch the tender flesh, but didn't dare. *Take care of them.* She nodded to the many girls in black who had swarmed up the ladder to stuff the attic, more girls than Orphelia had seen up here before.

Orphelia realized, then, that Hypatia intended to martyr herself. And, apparently, she was leaving her recruits in Orphelia's care. *Why me?*

But Hypatia shook her head, unable to say more for the pain. Orphelia helped her tie the scarf around her neck again. And then Hypatia beckoned the new recruits downstairs and they were gone, leaving Orphelia alone to wonder why she had been chosen as the caretaker of this ragtag motley. She lay down on the mattress again and realized she couldn't even smell the stink of it anymore. She wondered if the stink had become a part of her.

All this, she thought wryly, because she wouldn't marry Henry Carver.

~

Winifred collected her on the third day and threaded her arm through Orphelia's as they walked down the cobbled streets, like bosom friends rather than captor and captive. The fresh air, even reeking as it did of raw sewage and stagnant rainwater, was a balm to soothe Orphelia's restlessness.

Hypatia and her girls now numbered in the hundreds, and when Orphelia and her escort arrived, they had already taken control of the courtyard before the City Hall steps. A crowd had gathered, a crowd of hundreds, and more were arriving, attracted to the hustle and bustle like flies to a corpse. Hypatia stood on a wooden crate and untied her scarf, holding it in place as the sunset illuminated her black dress and ghostly white skin in gold and pink.

A policeman stood toward the back of the crowd, taller by a head than anyone else there. "You, get down from there," he called.

"Are you ready to see?" Hypatia asked. Her voice was as loud as any man's, but it made Orphelia gasp. It was higher, more musical, like the trill of a flute or a bird. It was beautiful, even if there was a pained rasp behind it.

The crowd thrust their arms into the air. They were mostly women, except for the police officers gathering around the edges of the throng, so their shouts were not so much a ringing chorus as a hiss, like the sound of a giant snake, with a few impassioned squeaks and choked grunts. A few reporters at the back of the crowd scribbled notes and an artist frantically sketched the scene in charcoal.

Hypatia pulled the scarf away with a triumphant flourish. Her throat was red, lumpy, purple and blue in places, green in others, horribly bruised and probably oozing something, but the sutures held. Her voice rang out. "If you take our voices," she pointed at the policemen now pulling batons from their belts. "We will take yours!"

The assembled women hissed their approval and Hypatia's scarf fluttered dramatically to the ground. Hypatia reached into her pocket and pulled out her trusty silver razor, lifting it high, so the sun's last rays limned it gold. Orphelia's breath caught. She was reminded of Durandar, Legbiter, and Excalibur.

Winifred had brought Orphelia close now, close enough that she could see Venus hovering directly behind Hypatia, waiting to catch her should she collapse. Arrayed around the crate on which she wobbled were a dozen girls in black, like dogs ready to attack. Orphelia turned to regard the crowd and watched as hoods and hats were thrown off, and black-clad women and girls turned their backs to Hypatia so they could face the police officers ringing the gathering. A tense silence fell over the courtyard for an instant as the sun slipped below the horizon, plunging them all into the hazy gray of early evening lit only by the dull golden glow of streetlamps.

A shot rang out, and blood erupted from Hypatia's throat, a long crimson scarf, nearly black in the darkness. She tumbled gracefully from the crate.

The riot began.

Winifred joined her sisters, a razor flashing in her hands as she rushed a policeman who fumbled with his pistol. Chaos exploded all around Orphelia. Unarmed, she could only stand watching as the revolutionaries and the police collided, razors versus batons, fists versus pistols. The men shouted curses and commands, but the women were silent, their voices stolen, their demands spoken in a language of blood and bruises.

Orphelia turned back to the crate where Hypatia's body lay sprawled. Venus was trying to drag her down. Orphelia ran to help, and together they pulled their leader's body to the ground. Venus sought a pulse at Hypatia's throat, her wrist. But she shook her head and lowered Hypatia's eyelids.

*They shot her,* Orphelia rasped.

*She chose her fate,* Venus answered.

*We need to get out of here.*

*Back to the attic. Do you know the way?*

Orphelia nodded and took off running up the City Hall steps, hoping she could perhaps discern a path back to the sidewalk through the riot from above.

Instead, she saw a familiar figure standing in the teeming crowd, perfectly still, her eyes locked on Orphelia. Orphelia blinked. It was her mother, Maude. Orphelia deflated for a moment, confused, fearful, expecting to see disappointment or perhaps even hatred in her mother's eyes.

But the only emotion on Maude's face was hope. She mouthed, *Me next.* Her hand fluttered to her throat.

Two futures spread out before Orphelia. In one, she married a doctor. In the other, she was the doctor.

She extended her hand to her mother and beckoned her to follow.

# DYLAN

Lorraine was finally certain Dylan wasn't her son on his fourth birthday. She had spent two years full of doubt and worry, watching her sweet baby boy transform into a child she didn't recognize. On that day, as he climbed the furniture, ignored his gifts, pushed other children out of the way, and shoved cake into his mouth with his fists like an infant, the sensation of certainty was the stab of a cold knife to her belly.

Her friends looked at her pityingly as they gathered their children and left her home. Dylan didn't notice, busy climbing the entertainment center and flinging himself onto the couch over and over. Alone with him, Lorraine stared despondently at the baby pictures given the place of honor on the mantle. Dylan took the opportunity to climb onto the kitchen counters and throw the dishes onto the kitchen floor. They were all plastic, as this was not the first time he had attempted this feat, but the sound of plastic bouncing on linoleum made Lorraine grind her teeth just the same.

When he fell asleep on the floor, his hands still gripping a cup and a fork, she carried him to bed and began cleaning up the mess. She dialed her grandmother while she cleaned. When

Nan answered, Lorraine sobbed into the phone for several minutes.

"He's not my son," she finally gasped.

Nan breathed a sigh that crackled down her landline. "*Die Wechselbalg.*"

Lorraine shook her head, stacking plastic plates on the shelf with shaking hands. "My friends say I should take him to the doctor, have him tested. But Nan, he's not the same boy."

"Your son was stolen from you." Nan's accent seemed thicker than usual, giving each vowel a deep, sonorous quality that made her words sound weighty and prophetic. "The *Fee* have taken him, and left *die Kreature* in his place."

Lorraine had been raised by her grandmother and knew just enough of Nan's native language to understand the mixture of English and German in which she often spoke. "Fairies?" Her stomach hurt with an ache like an open wound. "You think he's a changeling?"

"Yes, that is the problem. It used to be very common. Now not as much."

Lorraine paused to stare at her reflection in the window over the sink. Her eyes were sunken and shadowed, her mouth a thin line of worry, her skin sallow. Living with the thing she called Dylan, the thing that was not Dylan, was sucking the life out of her. "What can I do to get my boy back?"

"The *Fee* want a gift—no, more than that, *die Opfer*. I think the word is sacrifice. A gift that is a sacrifice."

"Like, a lamb or a chicken?"

"*Nein, nein.* Something that is a sacrifice for you. Something meaningful."

Tears pooled in Lorraine's eyes again. "I have nothing. Dylan is everything to me. What else can I give up?"

Silence hissed through the phone's speaker as both women pondered this question.

After a few moments, Nan's voice spoke again, and it was cold and sharp as a knife. "I know what we can bring."

Lorraine and her ex-husband Trevor had brought Dylan camping two years ago. This, Nan insisted, was where the trouble began, where they had attracted the attention of the fairies and the trade had been made. Lorraine and Trevor had left their son in the woods and taken home a fairy creation, all unwitting.

The thought made Lorraine want to throw up. She was nauseated the whole two-hour drive to the woods.

Beside her, Nan hummed traditional German folk songs. Lorraine had half-expected her to show up in a *dirndl*, but instead she wore jeans and her favorite blue puffy coat. Her white hair was styled into a long braid and covered by a burgundy beanie a friend had made her. She had brought them both coffee in thermoses, blankets, and an assortment of other items in a duffle bag.

In the backseat, the thing that wasn't Dylan squirmed and screamed in Dylan's car seat. It quieted down long enough to eat some chicken nuggets on the way, and then finally passed out for the remainder of the drive. Lorraine felt a pang of pity for it, and Nan caught her looking at her fraudulent son in the rearview mirror.

"It's not your boy," Nan whispered, glancing back at the sleeping thing that looked like a child.

"What will become of him–it?" Lorraine asked.

Nan shrugged. "Who cares? It's not real."

They arrived at the campsite close to sunset. The temperature was dropping precipitously as the light disappeared, and Lorraine tried to get a coat on the creature pretending to be her son. Not-Dylan slapped and kicked and squealed until finally she let him go. Holding his little coat in her hands, she watched him scramble up a nearby tree and wondered why she cared. He was an impostor, not her son. But, she supposed, that was the point, wasn't it? It was a thing that looked like a child, a thing that inspired adults to care for it, even when it was the cuckoo hatchling in their nest, tricking them. Still, she cared what became of the thing that was her enemy. How cleverly made it was. She secretly hoped it would have a happier life among the fairies, where no one would stop it from climbing as high as it could, or leaping from too-high branches, or eating with its hands and defecating wherever it wanted. It should have the freedoms it was denied among humans.

It couldn't help what it was. It wasn't the changeling's fault it had been made to take her son's place, sent home with her and Trevor to pretend to be a boy.

Nan pulled the duffel bag from the trunk and removed some items: candles, jewelry, a weathered deck of tarot cards, a few bundles of dried herbs, a plate from Nan's wedding china, and a white cashmere scarf. She arranged these items on a blanket near the tree line. Then she lit the candles, turned off her flashlight, and knelt beside this offering. She raised her hands and began to sing in German.

Lorraine knelt beside her. Behind them, she could hear Not-Dylan grunting and babbling as he climbed trees and jumped to the ground, then repeated the whole process. Tears stung her eyes, making hot tracks as they ran down her cheeks. Her breath frosted in the air on each exhale and she thought about bringing the changeling Dylan's coat. Do fairy creations get cold?

Footsteps approached them and the thing pretending to be a boy appeared beside her. He reached out one little hand and touched the tears shining on her cheeks. His breath smelled like chicken nuggets, hot enough to make a cloud in front of him like he was a real person. Suddenly, he collapsed to the ground and crawled into Lorraine's lap. She drew the coat over him and wrapped her arms around his little body instinctively.

"*Nein!*" Nan snapped, grabbing Lorraine's arm. Her eyes shone in the moonlight, pale and rheumy so they were like bright marbles in the darkness. "That's not Dylan. Don't forget!"

Lorraine nodded but her lungs felt too tight to contain the

conflicting emotions inside her. She could barely breathe. Tears spilled from her eyes, dripped off her jaw, and landed on the coat tucked around the now-sleeping changeling child.

Something in the forest moved, the tree branches trembling.

Nan raised her arms again and resumed her strange song. An icy wind stirred Lorraine's hair and she wished she'd worn a hat instead of just earmuffs. The candles guttered and threatened to go out.

"Light the herbs," Nan commanded, gesturing to the matches and herb bundles laid out on the blanket. Lorraine did as commanded, placing the burning herbs on the china plate decorated with dainty flowers. The scent of burning plants was strong and the changeling boy whimpered in her lap. She drew the hood over his head and held him close. He didn't deserve to be cold. There was no cause to be cruel, even if he wasn't her son.

Nan raised the jewelry and the scarf in her hands and held them up in offering, continuing to sing. With the warm creature in her lap, Lorraine became bored and sleepy and nodded off. Her eyelids were heavy and when she forced them open, determined to stay awake, her vision was blurry. Between long blinks, shapes moved in the trees: small, vaguely humanoid shapes, limned in silver moonlight.

Fear stabbed through her chest and brought her to full alertness. Nan, who must have heard her gasp, gave her a meaningful look.

"I saw something," Lorraine whispered. "I saw...shapes. There's something in the trees."

Nan raised her arms higher and sang louder. Lorraine knew the sounds of the song by now–though she didn't know the meaning of all the words–and she joined in, though her voice was tremulous and weak beside her grandmother's.

Finally, after what seemed like an eternity, something limped out of the trees and onto the blanket. It took Lorraine a few moments to process what she was seeing. She didn't know what she had expected to appear, but it wasn't a black vulture. Up close, it was bigger than she would have expected, with a head that looked too small for its body. The vulture looked at her with glassy black eyes and dug huge, sharp talons into the blanket. It smelled like death, and beetles swarmed around its feet. Lorraine drew back in revulsion.

Nan quieted and leaned forward, placing the offerings before the giant bird and pressing her forehead to the blanket.

In her head, Lorraine heard a voice. It didn't speak in German or English or in any language she had ever heard, but somehow she still understood, as if it spoke to her very bones. "It's been a long time since I heard that song," the voice said. It sounded amused or pleased, but there was also an edge of annoyance, as if it didn't like being pleased.

"Oh great *Feen Königin*, we bring you this offering to please you," Nan said, raising her head enough so that her voice could be heard. Lorraine wondered if she, too, should bow, but couldn't figure out how to do so around the body of the changeling draped over her lap. Like a real child, he was boneless in sleep and unbothered by the voices and movement around him.

The vulture limped forward with its weird, staggering gait and extended its long neck to sniff the jewelry and the scarf. The voice in her mind asked Lorraine, "Why?"

Lorraine swallowed, fear stealing her words. The vulture was very close to her now, and it was enormous, the size of a large dog. The beetles skittered close to her knees on at the edge of the blanket and she fought the urge to scream and flee.

"We want back the boy you took," Nan said, and once again her voice was cold and sharp. "The one you exchanged for this *Wechselbalg*."

The vulture made a sound, an ugly sound that startled Lorraine and nearly released her bladder. Its huge wings unfurled, and it shook them. The smell of decay became overpowering and Lorraine's eyes watered, her throat gagging.

"I did not take any boy from you," the mind-voice said. "But I will accept these gifts for troubling me."

The branches overhead rustled and several tiny humanoid creatures suspended on whirring wings dove down onto the blanket and snatched up the jewelry. The vulture grabbed the cashmere scarf with its beak, moving more swiftly than Lorraine would have thought possible for a creature of its bulk. The candles, burned almost down to nubs, flickered violently as the vulture flapped its massive wings and rose into the air, thankfully dispersing the odor of decomposition and death, though Lorraine wasn't sure she would ever stop smelling it completely.

"NO!" Lorraine screamed, leaping to her feet, pushing the changeling from her lap. "I want my son back!"

The vulture circled overhead, the scarf trailing behind it. The bird's silhouette passed over the moon a few times before it winged away. Silence settled over them. Lorraine wanted to weep, but she felt empty inside, hollow, as if there was no more sorrow to spare.

Nan said something in German, so softly Lorraine almost couldn't hear it. While her brain turned the words over and tried to translate them, something emerged from the trees. It was easily seven feet tall, and it was almost impossible to comprehend. It was white, stark in the darkness, practically glowing in the moonlight as if lit from within. It had the arms and hands of a human woman but its head, its body, and the antennae that twitched from its head were those of an insect, something familiar but never so large…a praying mantis. A mantis the size of a professional basketball player, with white faceted eyes and the arms and hands of a person. It was the strangest thing Lorraine had ever seen, and her knees buckled, sending her back to the ground, so that the enormous mantis towered over her, hands neatly folded, mandibles clicking.

"The bargain is struck," the voice in her mind said, and there was a finality to it, the tolling of a bell that rang only once a century, an ominous bell that could not be unrung. Lorraine understood that this was the source of the voice, and the vulture had only been her proxy. This terrifying vision was the fairy queen they had hoped to summon.

The mantis reached behind her and pulled from the forest a four-year-old boy. His clothes were rough and his hair long and tangled but it was Dylan. Lorraine would know her son's face, her son's eyes, her son's smile anywhere, any time, with only the tiniest sliver of light.

She ran to him and enfolded him in her arms. He smelled rank, like body odor and decay, like old meat and sweat. But he was her boy. Tears of relief flooded her eyes and she kissed his dirty, smelly face, heedless of the filth and stench. Then she embraced him again.

Dylan did not return her embrace. He stood stiffly, letting his mother fawn over him.

When Lorraine finally turned to thank the giant mantis who had granted her wish, she was gone. So was the changeling boy, leaving only an empty coat on the ground. And of course, Nan was gone, too. Lorraine finally understood her last words: *Take me as your sacrifice, only give her the boy she wants.*

Lorraine looked down at Dylan and smiled. He returned the expression hesitantly, as if he'd never smiled before. She took his hand in hers and held it tightly. "Are you ready to go home, sweetie?"

Dylan nodded and Lorraine's heart did a backflip when he said, "Yes, Mother."

"Gosh, Dylan seems so different," Gayle said, bouncing her new baby on her knee as she watched her daughter scrambling around the playground with Dylan. "I thought for sure he needed psychological testing. But now he seems fine."

Lorraine's mouth was suddenly dry and she sipped her iced

latte, her eyes tracking her son as he climbed the ladder and slid down the slide. "He's on a gluten-free, sugar-free diet."

Gayle made an appreciative sound. "That must be hard. I don't know what I'd do if I couldn't feed Kayleigh McDonald's!"

Lorraine offered her friend a smile that was closer to a grimace. "It's not easy, but it's worth it."

After one last time down the slide, Dylan walked over to his mother. His movements were so controlled, so confident–not like the other six-year-olds at the playground, who swayed and flailed and tripped on their own feet. And when he spoke, his voice was clear and words carefully enunciated, as if he'd had elocution lessons. "Mother, I'm ready to go home for lunch."

"So mature!" Gayle marveled.

Kayleigh, who had flung her tiny body from the swing set into the mulch and scraped her knee, began screaming. "MOMMY!" Gayle jumped up and ran over to her daughter.

The girl's screams making her shudder, Lorraine stood and took Dylan's hand. "Want to get an ice cream cone on the way?"

He smiled that soft, hesitant smile of his. "Yes, please."

Walking home, Dylan sedately licked his ice cream cone and Lorraine smoked a cigarette. She had never really understood the appeal of smoking until the last few months. Now she took every opportunity to draw the calming smoke into her lungs. Nicotine pushed down the anxiety threatening to devour her alive.

They arrived at their apartment building and Dylan held the door for her. They made their way up the stairs and into the apartment. Dylan didn't run or skip or jump or attempt to slide down the banister. It was like walking beside a very small adult. He threw away the bottom part of his ice cream cone in the trash, washed his hands without prompting, and removed his little peacoat, hanging it in the hall closet. He took off his shoes and placed them neatly on the shoe rack.

"Why don't you take a bath while I make lunch," Lorraine

suggested, moving into the kitchen, already longing for another cigarette.

"Yes, Mother." Dylan's sock feet padded into the bathroom.

Lorraine got out the bread, the peanut butter, a jar of grape jelly, a bag of chips. She arranged them on the counter. Her heart thumped hard and something lodged in her throat. She went back into the foyer and stared at Dylan's shoes on the shoe rack beside hers. They were nearly spotless despite a morning at the park.

His peacoat hanging in the closet was perfect, not even marred by fabric pills. She went into his bedroom and inspected the clothes he'd discarded in the hamper before going to take his bath. There was not a fleck of dirt, not a speck of blood or smear of snot. They smelled like him though, and she frowned. The Dylan she had brought back from the forest didn't smell right. The simulacrum of her son had smelled like sweet condensed milk and sometimes like sweaty socks. This Dylan smelled like brackish water and rotting flowers, and no matter how many baths she had him take, no matter how many times he changed his clothes, it never went away for long.

The walls in Dylan's room were covered with pages from coloring books, mostly images of superheroes, each colored so precisely there was not a crayon stroke out of place. Lorraine pressed her fingers against an image of Spiderman with particularly impressive shading. Dylan had only been in kindergarten for a few months, but already his kindergarten art teacher was impressed by his drawings. The teacher was so excited about Dylan's talent she had gifted him a set of drawing tools, watercolor paints, and a high-quality sketchbook.

Lorraine needed to find that sketchbook. She couldn't put into words why she had to find it, but she had a suspicion, an inkling, a seed of the truth digging at her brain waiting to sprout, and somehow she knew the contents of the sketchbook was very, very important to confirming or disproving this suspicion. She tore through Dylan's desk, his closet, his toy box, under his bed.

In the back corner of the shadowy space under his bed, she found an old Hot Wheels tin. She opened it to find it filled with dead insects, mostly flies and ladybugs. Her gorge rose and she snapped the lid back onto the tin and thrust it back under the bed as if it would burn her.

From where she knelt beside the bed, the lump made by the sketchbook hidden under the mattress became apparent.

Sitting on the edge of Dylan's bed, listening to the water running in the bathtub, she flipped through the pages. Each drawing was more impressive than the last. Each was also more disturbing than the last.

In charcoal and watercolor Dylan had drawn vultures, beetles, grubs and worms, fairies with the heads of ants and the wings of dragonflies, rotten logs crawling with yellow fungus, wolves with eyes reflecting the moonlight, and his queen. The giant white praying mantis with a woman's arms was less detailed than the others, a quick sketch in charcoal, somehow infused with a sense of sadness, regret, and longing, as if he couldn't bear to render her on the page though he was compelled to do so.

The water in the bathtub stopped running. Lorraine considered hiding the sketchbook and going to the kitchen to finish assembling the sandwiches, but she couldn't move. Her whole body trembled.

Dylan emerged from the bathroom wearing clean clothes, his wet hair matted to his head. He paused in the doorway to his bedroom, staring at the sketchbook in Lorraine's hands, his jaw working but no sound emerging from his mouth.

"Do you miss her?" Lorraine asked, holding up the page with the white mantis.

Dylan heaved a sigh and stared at his toes. "No, Mother."

Lorraine patted the bed next to her. "I think it's best if we're honest with each other."

The boy didn't move, but he did raise his head. Tears sparkled in his eyes. "Have I disappointed you?"

Lorraine's lungs constricted. "What? No. You've been a perfect son."

"You don't want me anymore?"

She shook her head, glancing back down at the sketchbook. She turned the page, and there was a sketch of a familiar woman. Dylan had drawn Lorraine with sunken cheeks and a cigarette held between slender fingers. It was the first time she realized how much weight she'd lost, how skeletal she'd become, since that night in the woods. "I don't know what I want," she admitted softly. "What do you want?"

Dylan pressed his lips together, his eyes widening. Had anyone ever asked him that question before? He looked stunned. "I want to make my queen happy."

"And she told you to be the perfect son."

"The boy you wanted."

Lorraine closed the sketchbook. "And if I don't want you anymore, she'll be disappointed."

He nodded.

"What if I traded you for my Dylan?" Her voice caught when she said his name.

The boy shook his head. "It's not the same. A child is worth more than anything, to her."

"What about my Nan?"

He shrugged. "Maybe."

Lorraine nodded and placed a trembling hand over her mouth. "I'm going to return you to the queen. You fulfilled your mission, but I want my son back. The real Dylan."

"I thought you didn't want him," the boy said. "I thought you wanted him to be like me."

Lorraine pressed her lips together hard, trapping the sobs that rose in her throat. "I did."

~

As soon as night fell, the queen's creatures came for the new Dylan. The bug-faced fairies tugged him by his shirt toward the trees where crows and owls perched, watching. Just before he disappeared, the boy looked back at Lorraine, and his face was no longer human. His eyes were huge and yellow, his nose was just two holes in the middle of his face, and his mouth became thin-lipped and filled with teeth like needles.

Lorraine waved goodbye anyway.

She opened the back door of the car and took out the Hot Wheels tin he'd left on the backseat. It was empty now. All pretense lost, he had snacked on crunchy fly corpses much of the drive to the campsite. She threw the tin on the ground and shivered.

The child seat still stank of rot and decay, so she unhooked it from the car and dumped it in the grass. One more item remained on the backseat: his sketchbook. He had sketched furiously with colored pencils the whole drive, and now Lorraine finally got to see the product of his labor. She clicked on the overhead light to get a better look at the new drawing.

It was the most colorful of the drawings in the sketchbook. He had drawn a brown-skinned woman, curvaceous, with heavy breasts and thick thighs, wearing only a crown of flowers, barefoot and standing in a field of wildflowers, surrounded by baby animals–fawns and kittens and baby bunnies. The fairies hovering over her shoulders had butterfly wings and human faces.

The woman's expression was suffused with joy. Above her, written in handwriting so neat it looked like a font, were two words: *Queen Antaria.*

Lorraine glanced back at the tree line. For a fleeting instant, she swore she saw two familiar shapes in the moonlight: a boy and an old woman, peering at her wide-eyed before they disappeared into the darkness.

# TAKE THE FIRE FROM HER

Felicity's fire was merely a spark when she was a babe, a useful skill for a girl whose parents were settlers. They had no need of flint or tinder after her first birthday. They liked to show her off to the cowboys who passed through, painting her ability as a gift rather than a curse, especially when she could light blazing bonfires during the howling gales common in the Kansas spring.

True, she did sometimes set her clothes on fire, and once burned down the cabin, but the clothes were made from flour sacks anyway, and the cabin the family built to replace the original was far roomier and sturdier. And as she grew, Felicity was better able to control the fire, so there was no more worry about setting the grasslands ablaze by accident.

Mama and Papa had more children, but none of them possessed Felicity's gift with fire. They were relieved. One of her kind was enough for the family, thank you very much, and they'd been lucky it was an obedient girl-child. Could you imagine if her brother Jedediah had such a power? He could barely piss in the latrine hole without getting it all over his trousers.

Around the time she turned fourteen, Felicity woke in the

night to her bed on fire. She ran outside and the family doused the burning bed with the bucket of water they kept in the bedroom for just such an occasion. Felicity burned for hours in the yard, her nightgown blackening and turning to ash. The fire had never hurt her before, but now it was like a thousand wasps stinging her all at once. She screamed and howled and rolled naked on the ground, desperate to make it stop.

Her family stood around her, throwing buckets of water and blankets over the flames, but the water evaporated and the blankets vaporized instantly in the heat of the six-foot-tall blue flames. They were reduced to putting out the small fires erupting in the grass nearby, waiting for Felicity to stop burning. For hours she wailed and cried and begged for them to help her.

Sometime in the mid-morning, the fire waned, the flames growing smaller until they finally went out, leaving behind a sobbing, soot-covered girl, thick gray smoke drifting up from her body, curled in the fetal position. All around her the earth was black, the grass seared away.

The poor girl was bald, right down to her eyelashes. The top layer of her skin was black and crispy to the touch. Over the next days and weeks, it would gradually peel away, revealing skin underneath as smooth and pink as a babe's. Her hair would grow back lustrous and golden. Her eyelashes returned longer and fuller. Even her gray eyes seemed bluer after that night.

The family built a special sleeping shed for Felicity after that, far from the main house, in an area cleared of grass. Just in case.

When cowboys and caravans of settlers visited the homestead, Felicity's gift was no longer what they noticed about her. Whispers began in town that Felicity was a witch. A carnival troupe passed through and offered ten whole dollars for her. Ten dollars was a lot, enough to feed the family for years, but Felicity's mother refused to sell. Her daughter was, after all, only a child, and she'd seen the look of lust on the ringleader's ugly face. She might be a witch, but she was still her mother's only daughter, and her first child.

One night, a cowboy snuck into Felicity's locked sleeping shed. She burned down the shed with him inside and would tell no one what had occurred, suddenly stricken with muteness. The local sheriff didn't know what to make of it. A posse of the cowboy's friends came for Felicity, but when they tried to grab her, she burst into blue flames. One tried to shoot her, but the bullets melted in the heat before they could touch her. Felicity burned and burned until the cowboys gave up.

After that, Felicity did as she pleased. She lived in the woods. Sometimes she would venture to the farmhouse with a skirt full of mushrooms or herbs and would eat dinner with her family. Other times they didn't see her for weeks. Some nights, her brother Jedediah would look out the window to see a bright blue spot glowing in the trees: his sister Felicity consumed by fire.

Desperate for help, Mama wrote to a faith healer advertised in the *Farm & Feed* catalogue.

Three months later, on a cold October day, Reverend Hightower stepped onto the farm. He was a tall man dressed in austere black, with a tall black hat and a huge black horse. He looked less like a faith healer, Mama thought, and more like a demon hunter.

Felicity emerged naked from the woods to greet him. Her lustrous hair was a matted tangle full of sticks and leaves. Her beautiful skin was caked with mud and crisscrossed with streaks of blood. But her eyes, her eyes were bright blue, fierce and full of fire.

Reverend Hightower promised he could take the fire from her. Mama wept with relief. Papa sent the other children to fetch buckets of water and soaked blankets, because he was a practical man. Felicity knelt before the Reverend, her head held high.

The Reverend walked around to her back and placed his hand against her skin. Flames erupted where he touched. He gritted his teeth and did not pull his hand away. The family watched in wonder as he burned while uttering a strange prayer in a language that sounded like Latin but wasn't Latin, not any

Latin Papa had heard, and he'd spent his formative years in Catholic school.

When Reverend Hightower finally pulled his hand away, the fire came with it. Felicity screamed, long and low, the sound a cow makes when she loses her calf to wolves. The Reverend clenched his fist and the fire consumed his hand. He released a shout of agony as his skin blackened and peeled away down to the bone, but the fire died.

Felicity curled in on herself, collapsing to the ground. Mama ran to her, wrapping her arms around her precious baby girl and pleading with her not to die, yet Felicity breathed no more. The sound Mama made was so terrible the air seemed to waver and shrink back from her sorrow.

Papa's hands went to the Reverend's throat, but Reverend Hightower was gone. What stood in his place was a creature out of myth, a thing in the shape of a man, but with eyes of burning coal and a mouth full of needle-teeth. The thing disguised as Reverend Hightower laughed and executed a bizarre, boneless jig, mounting the horse that was now a skeletal nightmare. The sound of the demon's rasping, grating laughter hovered over the farm long after his silhouette had receded on the horizon.

The family buried Felicity in the forest. Every October, Mama and Papa woke in the night to see something bright in the trees. The ghost never came to the house, and she disappeared when Mama ran to her.

After Mama and Papa passed, it was Jedediah and his wife who saw the blue fire between the branches.

Jed wasn't surprised when one of his daughters had the spark.

# NANA

You sit with your feet dangling in the black water, kicking at a plastic bottle, when the latest drop crashes to the beach. The delivery ship jets away across the gray sky, and you're up and running like a dozen other kids, leaping over old tires and bounding across mounds of reeking refuse. A fresh drop means unpicked treasures, and whoever gets there first will have first choice.

You scale the mountain of garbage and wade through knee-high detritus searching for a prize. There's no competition among the children, not like there is between adults. You're not after items to trade or build, you're after items to collect. You call to Arin to see the holographic baseball card you found wedged between two glass bottles. It's sticky and one he already has, but duplicates are more exciting than nothing. You bring Rissa an action figure to add to her collection. The legs are missing, but she's delighted. She can always splice it together with a torso and a random head to create a finished hero.

"We're gonna throw stuff down the whirlpool later, if you want to come," Rissa offers.

You shrug. You desperately want to go, but you have responsibilities now that you're old enough to contribute to the household. "I have to look for books later, for Mother. The whirlpool is for little kids, anyway."

Rissa narrows her eyes at you and then scurries away.

Afternoon humidity sets in and most of the other kids drift away to enjoy their finds. Your energy wanes in the heat, and the pile of fresh trash starts to stink. Your stomach aches, ready for a midday meal. You turn to climb down the pile and something slick slides out from under your foot and you're thrown off balance. You fall, sliding and rolling down the incline, and the trash heap shifts around you. Your heart hammers when you slide to a stop halfway down, awaiting an avalanche, certain that you're about to meet the same end as so many pickers before you, buried beneath a mountain of steaming garbage.

The trash settles and you breathe a sigh of relief. As you scramble to your feet, ready to inch your way carefully home, something catches your eye, something fabric, stained but originally flesh-colored. You grab for it, excitedly at first, and then more cautiously, slowly pulling your treasure from the mound so as not to disturb it again.

The object is a doll. She is made of beige fabric, now stained a filthy gray, the same color as the sludge water that taints everything here. Her eyes were once buttons, but they went missing long ago, leaving behind only two pieces of discolored brown felt. Her mouth is stitched on in a wide smile that, combined with the missing eyes, gives the impression of a grimace. Her hair is little more than a few frayed strands of yarn. She's clothed in a dress that might once have been lavender with tiny purple flowers, and her shoes have been painted on, still glossy and black.

She's exactly the treasure you hoped to find. You clutch her to your chest and rush home, heedless of the dangers in the sliding garbage beneath your bare feet.

You climb the ladder to your house with the doll tucked under your arm. You and your mother live in a house built on stilts to protect it from the dangerous tides that threaten to sweep the whole community away during the monsoon season. Your house is not the largest, but you have no brothers and sisters with whom you must share your tiny bedroom, so there's no one to resent your doll collection. You straighten the new doll's dress and present her to the others, arrayed all over your bedroom. In your collection there are mostly baby dolls and a few fashion dolls, as their plastic shells are the most likely to survive decay. Most are naked, many are missing limbs or eyes, others are merely watchful heads without bodies to support them. But you know all their names, all their personalities, their likes and dislikes, and which dolls get along with which others.

"This is...Nana," you announce, holding up the new doll so each of the others can get a good look. "I expect you all to be on your best behavior." The room is crowded, but you find a spot on the mattress where you can place the newest addition to your collection. Nana grimaces up at you.

The midday meal is shrimp dredged up from the bottom of the ocean, the meat gray and sludge-flavored. Your mother offers you half a piece of fruit from that morning's picking, a rare and fantastic thing, and you savor the delicate sweetness of it, the soft texture, the edge of rot giving it a sour aftertaste.

You return to your room for a rest after the meal, curled up on your mattress stuffed with bits of fabric from the trash heaps, and you dream of Nana. She is whole, with bright button eyes and red yarn hair braided down her back in two neat plaits. She stares and smiles, and you hold her hand, and you skip through a field of wildflowers. You know what a field is because of the books your mother brings home from the heaps, but you've never experienced a wide-open space full of flowers, with a blue sky above you. Everything here on Tethis IV is gray, gray and brown and black and stinking. In your dream, the air is clean and smells sweet, and you hear birdsong in the distance. There are colors here you rarely see, pale pinks and bright yellows. You wake with tears in your eyes for a life you never knew you wanted.

Mother shakes you awake. "It's alright. You're safe," she says, her brow creased with worry.

It's rare for Mother to touch you, and rarer still for her to look at you with concern etched in her features. "It wasn't a bad dream," you say. "Nana and I were playing in a field of flowers. They smelled so good."

She frowns at the doll pressed against your chest. "This is Nana?"

You hold up your prize proudly. "I found her this morning."

Mother recoils, disgusted. "She's even filthier than the last one."

"That's not her fault," you say. "Everything here is filthy."

Mother reacts as if she's been slapped. It is, after all, her fault you both have to live on this awful trash planet. She's the one who was exiled to Tethis IV, alone except for you, without a partner to help her raise you. Her expression hardens again into the mask of indifference she usually wears, and she leaves your bedroom.

You feel guilty for making Mother unhappy, and spend the afternoon picking the new heap for books, Nana tucked under your arm. You find enough texts to fill the largest canvas bag you can carry and bring them home when the monsters start to roil the depths in preparation for evening, driving all the pickers inland.

Mother isn't home. You light the only lantern and sit on the floor, dumping books out around you to explore their pages. Most of the children of Tethis IV can't read, but your mother made sure you could read, and read well. It was, she said, one of life's greatest pleasures, and there were so few pleasures here. Mother's trade in books had, of late, suffered due to the illiteracy of the other exiles. She used to trade books for food, fuel, fabric, and whatever else you needed with ease, because the other exiles were hungry for new titles. Lately, though, demand had dried up. She had a theory it was because many of the exiles who could read had died or had their sentences commuted, and fewer prison ships were landing here each year, their human cargoes diminished.

You only know of what happens beyond your filthy shores thanks to the gossip new exiles bring. Most of it is meaningless and holds little interest for you. Tethis IV is all you've ever known, except for what you've learned in Mother's precious books. Sometimes she lets you read the nicest ones before she trades them. She has kept a few of her favorites on a shelf above the door, a handful of her most treasured texts, and you've read them with her so many times you've memorized the pages.

You prop Nana beside you and flip through the new books, looking for pictures. One is a dictionary, with a few drawings of plants and animals you've never seen. You find a medical text with fascinating anatomy illustrations. There's a small red journal, leather-bound, and very unlike the others. The pages are handwritten, and there are sketches of people and places. The journal falls open to a sketch of Nana, as you saw her in the dream, with buttons for eyes and her hair styled in two neat plaits.

A chill makes you shiver. Out of the corner of your eye, you see Mother at the door. You look up, and the shape of a woman dissolves into shadow. Panic flutters behind your breastbone. You pick up Nana and the journal and go to your room, shutting the door. You feel safe surrounded by the dolls, watching and protecting you. You slip the journal under your mattress and go to sleep with Nana tucked under your chin.

You dream again, this time of playing with Nana in a big, clean house. You're wearing clean, soft clothes, and your hair is freshly washed and curled and full of colorful ribbons. A tall, pale woman clothed in black smiles down at you, but her eyes are sad. She loves you, but death hangs around her like a shroud. She is sad the same way your mother is sad, and you take her hand and tell her you love her, trying to chase away the ghosts that mar her lovely face.

When morning comes, Mother makes you a breakfast of

something she calls "grits." From the descriptions you've read in cookbooks, this viscous substance is nothing like grits, but it's made from the only edible plant that grows on Tethis IV, which the exiles cultivate and trade. It tastes sour and has a lumpy, gooey texture. It's not your favorite meal, but it does fill you up and make your stomach feel warm and satisfied. Mother must have found some valuable books, or someone who found books valuable. It has been months since you've enjoyed a breakfast so decadent.

After breakfast, Mother begins sorting the books you found to take them for trade. You retreat to your room to thumb through the journal. You're particularly interested in the pages that talk about the doll. The journal's author also calls her Nana, a fact that makes your hands tremble as you turn the pages. The author writes about her vivid dreams, where she lives in another time, in another place, on Old Earth. She sketches the field of wildflowers and the face of the pale woman in black.

You drop the journal to the floor and kick it away from you at the sight of the woman's face. How did you know the doll was named Nana? How did the author of this journal draw what was in your dreams? Who is the woman in black? You stare down at Nana, unsure what to do. She grimaces up at you, her smile suddenly malevolent. You need space and time to think. You open the door and take her into the main room of the house, placing her on the shelf above the door with your mother's most precious books. Then you hurry out of the house, off to the trash heaps, where you do your best thinking while looking for treasures.

Hours later, you return to the house with a broken chair and part of a coffee pot. Mother is pleased, as she thinks she'll be able to trade them both. There's no fruit for the midday meal, but there is bread. It's gritty and has a bitter flavor because the flour is made from ground-up insects, but it's nutritious.

Nana is no longer above the door. You assume Mother must have gotten rid of her. You find yourself relieved, and then you feel a pang of guilt for feeling relieved. When you go in your room, you find that Nana sits on the bed, and now she has eyes that gleam in the dirty gray light. You scream.

"I thought I'd surprise you," Mother says, her hands fluttering in distress. "I found the buttons this morning. They're real abalone shell."

You nod slowly and twist your face into a smiling shape. "They're beautiful." Your pulse gallops and you hope Mother doesn't notice.

Mother goes out to pick in the afternoon. You tell her you don't feel well and you want to stay in. She has books for you to sort while she's gone, but while you work you can feel Nana's pearlescent eyes watching you. The red journal calls to you where you left it on the floor. Eventually the presence of both is oppressive. You go into your room and pick them up, ready to toss them out the window.

But held in your hands, Nana is just a handmade doll, and the journal is just an old, crumbling book. Why are you so afraid? It seems silly, now, your fear. You sit on your mattress and your doll collection watches as you seat Nana in your lap and open the journal. The author found Nana in something called an "antique shop." The doll has "Nana" stitched on her behind, so that must be her name, and you reason that you must have glimpsed the embroidered tattoo, and that's how you knew what to call her.

Nana and the author became inseparable. The author began to have vivid dreams, and then started seeing the pale woman in black during her waking hours, always out of the corner of her eye. She had a dream about the woman trying to kill her, to drown her.

An old newspaper clipping falls out of the journal. You unfold it carefully and try to read it, but the ink is faded and the paper yellowed, so you can pick out only a few words: infanticide, disappeared, scandal. You'll need to look them up in the dictionary above the door to learn their meanings. There is a photograph, an image that makes your pulse beat hard. It's the face of the woman in the black dress. She isn't wearing black and she looks happier than she did in your dream, but it's the same woman. She holds a child in her lap, a child a little younger than you, with pale curls and bright eyes.

The author decided to return Nana to the antique shop in hopes of ending the frightening dreams. The journal pages after that are full of nonsensical scrawling and a drawing of huge, angry, black eyes.

You tuck the journal back under your mattress and gaze into Nana's shiny button eyes. They're so bright and colorful against the filthy brown of the felt, the stained beige of her fabric skin. They don't look right. You think how pretty they would be sewn onto your own shirt or woven into your hair, how Arin and Rissa would be jealous. And then maybe Nana wouldn't be able to stare at you anymore.

You rip the buttons from her face and spend the afternoon in front of your mother's small mirror, figuring out the best way to tie the buttons into your long, tangled hair. A few times you swear there's a shadow behind you in the mirror, a shadow in the shape of a woman in a black dress, but when you turn, it's gone. The journal calls to you from under the mattress, but you ignore it. You consider burning it so it will leave you alone.

Mother returns with fish, and you help her prepare it for dinner. She doesn't comment on your new adornments, or the fact that Nana is now eyeless and perched once again above the door. Mother is in one of her sullen moods, so you eat the fish in silence. Then she chooses a book from the stacks on the floor and disappears into her bedroom.

You choose a book yourself and stay up as long as you can, reading by lantern light, reluctant to sleep. Eventually your eyes close and you find yourself once again in the big, clean house, wearing soft, clean clothes. The pale woman in the black dress smiles down at you, but tears sparkle in her eyes. Her hands close around your neck, squeezing the breath from you. You try to pry her fingers from your throat but her slender digits are surprisingly strong. She thrusts your head underwater, and when you gasp for air, water fills your lungs, and the last thing you see is the woman standing over you, sobbing, her image distorted by the water.

You wake gasping for air, but something is pressed over your face. You struggle and squirm and the thing pressed over your face jerks back. Mother crouches by your mattress, holding her pillow, which bears the indentation of your face. She shakes her head, as if trying to wake herself. You scramble away from her, into the piles of dolls. You shake and suck down great gulps of air.

"I'm sorry," Mother says softly. "I don't know how I got here." She glances around, as if the room will somehow reveal the source of her sleepwalking. Her eyes light on Nana, and she runs from the room.

You gather up Nana and the red journal and climb down the ladder in the dark. Tethis IV has two moons: tonight Arisia is a pale sliver and her brother Boros, far across the sky, is almost full, providing most of the pale, silvery light. High above the garbage, a few houses provide additional pinpoints of illumination, but it's late. Almost everyone is sleeping.

The beach is silent except for the rushing of the waves and the pounding of your own heart. No one goes out at this time because of the monsters lurking just off the shore. They have long arms and can snatch trash pickers from a hundred feet away, so you creep carefully as far from the shore as you can until you arrive at the inlet caves.

The caves are a place where you and your friends have played many times—or you did, until you became old enough to pick trash and contribute to the livelihoods of your families. The moonlight can't reach inside the caverns, so you quickly find yourself shrouded in darkness. You feel your way along the familiar walls, following the flow of ankle-deep water, breathing the nostalgic aroma of cool earth and stone. You walk slowly, and your muscles start to shake from being tensed for so long. Your teeth chatter.

You feel as if you've been walking for hours when you finally come upon the whirlpool. The whirlpool is the reason the caves stay mostly free of trash. Everything that ends up in the caves gets sucked into the whirlpool and comes up elsewhere in the ocean unless it's strong enough to fight the current or someone has fastened it to the cave walls. Throwing things into the whirlpool is a fun activity for younger children. You remember losing several dolls into the swirling water before you understood they wouldn't come back.

You can't see the whirlpool but you can hear it rushing and feel the salty spray of it against your cheeks. You take a deep breath and heave both Nana and the red journal into the water. You don't hear a splash or anything else that would indicate their disappearance, but you swear you feel unwatched for the first time in days, as if the eyes on the back of your head have finally gone away.

You go home to find Mother sitting in the main room of the house, sobbing, her face red and snot-streaked. Several of your dolls are piled in her lap. When you enter, she jumps to her feet and spills the dolls to the floor, rushing to you with open arms. "I'm so sorry," she wails.

"It's okay," you say, returning her embrace. "It wasn't you. It was Nana. She's gone now. Everything is going to be okay."

As Mother weeps against your shoulder, you actually believe that maybe, just maybe, things really will be okay.

The long days of summer stretch into monsoon season. The rain pounds down, and you and Mother spend most of your time reading and sorting the books you stockpiled during the dry season. For an hour each morning you go to trade and find food and even do a little picking with your friends before the storms start again, but otherwise, you're trapped indoors. The house sways frighteningly on its stilts, sometimes, but they hold for another year.

Truth be told, it's your favorite time of year. Toward the end of the season, you have to reduce your rations, so your stomach hurts. But you and Mother spend a lot of time together and develop a quiet, pleasant rhythm. You absorb the stories in dozens of books, each one opening a world far away from Tethis IV. The storms smell of fresh water and tamp down the stink of the landfill that surrounds you. The gray days run together into one cozy, hazy, endless stretch of time.

Finally, the first day of the new summer season announces itself with clear skies. Birds wheel overhead and you venture out with your friends to hunt them with spears and arrows. The birds aren't particularly good eating, but it's a relief to eat something until your shrunken stomach is full, and tracking them across the trash dunes is a fun exercise after so long cooped up indoors.

You're with Arin and Rissa, tracking a bird to its nest in the hopes of stealing its eggs, when you find yourself at the inlet caves. "Let's go see the whirlpool," Arin suggests, his eyes twinkling.

A feeling of dread simmers in your stomach. "Isn't that for babies?"

Arin shrugs. "I just haven't been down there in a long time."

"I go all the time," Rissa says. "It's nice. I like the sound of it, and the smell. The younger kids don't hang out there like we did, not anymore, not since Duggy fell in."

You all take a few moments to think about the tragedy when Duggy, one of Rissa's cousins, fell into the whirlpool and the parents made the kids promise never to go there again. Naturally, the younger children keep their promises, but your mother never made you promise anything, and Rissa has eight brothers and sisters, so nobody keeps track of her. And Arin takes any parental order as a challenge, every rule as something to be broken.

You can't think of any further objections, so you follow your friends into the caves. Rissa has a flashlight cobbled together out of a bunch of electrical parts and a half-corroded battery. The light is dim but it's better than nothing.

The smell of the caves, the feel of the wet stone against your fingers, the slosh of your feet in the ankle-deep water, all brings you back to the night you disposed of Nana and the red journal. It's been so many months, the whole event seems hazy and unreal, especially since so much of it happened in total blackness. Your throat burns and you have a hard time taking deep breaths in the caves, as if the memory of the pale woman's hands around your neck has physical substance here.

Arin walks in the front, and he lets out an exclamation, the sound of which is nearly drowned out by the rushing of the whirlpool. Rissa splashes up to him, shining the flashlight on whatever he's found, and you follow, but slowly, reluctantly, dread making your feet leaden. You reach them and look down, expecting to see Nana lying there, soaked and filthy but intact.

It's a chunk of plastic with wires sticking out. You breathe a sigh of relief, your vision briefly filling with stars. "This is stupid," you say. "I'm leaving." You turn and head for the entrance, retracing your way in the dark. Behind you, Arin and Rissa's laughter echoes.

You spend your afternoon digging in the freshest trash heap near the water. It already stinks, as there's a lot of food waste, but you find a few oranges that are only half-moldy, and a couple of almost-black bananas. You make your way home excited to present your finds to Mother. She's been much less sullen, these past few months, and surely her spirits will be buoyed by the nice weather.

The house looks like it was hit by a monsoon. The meager furniture is smashed, your dolls thrown about, some of them dismembered. The little mirror is shattered and you cut your feet stepping on the shards of glass before you notice them. The books have been flung about the room and torn to bits, and one looks as if it has scorch marks on it. Mother is nowhere to be found. What could have happened?

You climb down the ladder and go to the neighbor's house to inquire after Mother. Your feet bleed on their rug. They haven't seen your mother, they don't know who ransacked your house, and they offer you bandages for your feet, but you don't have time for bandages. As evening approaches, you limp to the shore, but your mother isn't among the pickers coming in from the beach.

You go home, finally clean your stinging feet, and start setting things right around the house. A few times, you think you see your mother in the doorway, but the shadow is gone when you turn. You arrange the dolls in your room, taking comfort from the familiarity of the activity, brushing their hair and wiping smears of dirt from their cheeks. You fall asleep curled among them, waiting for Mother.

You dream of Mother holding you down, drowning you. Her face is pale and she wears a black dress. She cries and her face is distorted by the water, her tears making the surface ripple. You splash and struggle but she's strong, and your lungs fill with fluid, and darkness overtakes you. Your chest aches and then you feel nothing.

When you gasp to wakefulness, a woman is silhouetted in your doorway. It might be your mother, but it doesn't really look like her, and she's wearing a long dress, unusual clothing for Tethis IV. Something misshapen dangles from her right hand. In her left, something rectangular. She steps into the room and the moonlight briefly limns her form, picking out details: the doll gripped in her right hand, the journal clutched in her left. Her face is pale and twisted, but it is Mother, you think. But it's also...not Mother. Like someone else is wearing Mother's skin.

You crab-walk away from her, backing yourself into the corner, pulling your dolls over you, trying to hide. Her head turns, slowly, gaze fixing on you. She drops the doll and the journal, and then she steps to the wall, scaling it like a lizard you saw once in a book. She climbs across the ceiling until she dangles directly above you. Terror paralyzes you as she leans down over you, somehow still clinging to the ceiling, her face appearing in front of yours, upside-down, her long hair dangling so that it brushes your lap. Her eyes are black and her brows drawn together in a way you've never seen before. She's so angry the rage practically pours off her.

You manage to choke out three words: "Who…are…you?"

She says only one word in reply: "Nana." The voice is not your mother's. It's too low, too rough, like something dredged up from the depths of the black ocean.

"I want my mother," you say.

She laughs, a sound like a door creaking wetly. "Your mother never loved you. She never wanted you. You were an accident, a mistake. You got her exiled here. She hated you before you were even born. She wishes you were dead, so she could leave this place."

Her hands reach for your throat. You sink back into the dolls and she grabs at them instead. She screams in frustration, tossing dolls everywhere, snarling and scrabbling at them. You slide into and under your collection, crawling and wriggling until you emerge on the other side of the room. You run for the door. Your mother hisses and follows you, her knees and hands thumping against the ceiling as she crawls above you.

You snatch the Nana doll and the red journal out of the doorway as you pass through it. The lantern is on the shelf by the door, the matches beside it. You throw the doll and the journal into a basket full of books. You open the lantern and pour the oil over the contents of the basket, your hands shaking so hard you can barely manage the cap. Oil goes everywhere, on the floor, on your clothes. But it lands on the basket, too, on the doll and the journal.

There's a thump behind you. Your heart pounds and your

breath comes in great, ragged gasps, inhaling the scent of the oil, the reek of the rotting trash planet. Everything slows as you turn to face your mother.

Mother reaches for your throat again, and this time she has you. She slams you against the wall, crushing your windpipe with her powerful grip. You squirm and kick but she's so strong. Your lungs burn and darkness gnaws at the edges of your vision. Your hands flail and find a book, bringing it up to slap the side of Mother's face with it. She ignores it until you drive the corner of the book into her eye. Shrieking, she releases you to bat the book away.

You push her off you, grabbing for the matches and turning to the basket. Her hands close around your neck from behind but not before you strike a match, not before a small flame flares to life, not before you drop it into the basket.

The oil catches fire instantly. Mother screams with a terrible, otherworldly shriek as the doll burns. She tears at you, trying to get to the basket, but you stand firm, holding her at bay. Suddenly you're the strong one.

The room fills with the smell of burning fabric and something else, something sharp and smoky and evil-smelling. Mother wilts before you, collapsing to the floor. Her shriek becomes a wail, and that fades to a despairing murmur.

You kneel beside her, pulling her into your embrace. "I want my mother."

Her face twists with rage one last time. She coughs. Her eyelids flutter. The rage leaves her body like juice from a rotten fruit, and she sags in your arms. Her breathing slows. She relaxes into something that resembles normal sleep.

You stomp out the fire. Fire on a landfill spreads with incredible speed, and you can't risk starting a conflagration that might kill everyone you know. You carry the remnants of the basket down the ladder. You carry it to the caves in the dark, as you did once before, but now, you walk with confidence. You know this place so well, and you traversed it in darkness once before. You see no reason to be afraid. In the cave, you place the basket and its contents on a ledge and light another match. This time you let the bundle burn down until the fire goes out on its own.

You take what's left, mostly ash, and fling it into the whirlpool. You light a match so you can watch it swirl down into the dark water. Then you begin the long, dark trek back to the house, where you know you'll find your mother.

You wonder, as you walk, whether things will go back to how they were, or whether things will be different. Nana's words haunt you. Was your mother exiled here because of you? Does she hate you? Your heart is heavy with exhaustion and sorrow.

As you approach the house, you see a candle burning in your bedroom window, and the shape of your mother moving around the room. She's rearranging the dolls, trying to put your collection back in place, trying to erase the damage Nana did.

You smile, and you think of how much the little kids will love your dolls when you give them away.

# THE LAST MONSTER OF THE NINE REALMS

## 1

I scrub at the paint marring the tombstone with all the vigor I can muster. My hands don't feel the bitter chill of winter, but my joints cramp and protest just the same. I grit my teeth against the sharp stabs of arthritis in my fingers and knees and continue scouring, determined to obliterate the defacement. Eventually, however, my hands curl into claws and I drop the brush, unable to continue.

Leaning against the rough stone, I let myself release a few silent tears. They freeze on my cheeks.

The dense quiet is broken by the crunch of boots on snow. My lungs fill with the familiar scents of leather and sweat and brass. I know the identity of the interloper before I turn to see her, even though thirty years have elapsed between our last meeting and this one.

"Devora," I breathe, the sound whisked from my lips by the icy wind. I stagger to my feet and turn to blink up at my old friend.

Devora is as I remember her: tall, pale, broad-shouldered, dressed in rune-etched armor and a cloak the color of fresh blood. Her hair is silver instead of black, and the right side of her face is scarred with the twisted flesh of old burns. Her right eye is a sightless white orb, but the left one is just as hard and bright as I recall. She fixes me with it, and I can see from her expression that I've changed too.

"Narienne Lore," she says, and the sound of my name from her lips sends a thrill through my body.

"Not what you expected?" I feel self-conscious about my stooped shoulders and white hair for the first time.

Devora grins. Something inside my chest flutters at the sight of her smile. "We've become old women."

"Some of us have done better in our old age than others, General Devora. I'm sad to say you're a week late for Jax's funeral." I pat my husband's tombstone.

"I'm sorry for that. You know I always liked and respected Jax. He was one of the last great monster hunters. But that's not why I'm here."

I narrow my eyes at her, kicking the scrub brush across the frozen grass to bump the toe of her boot. "Scrub while you talk, General."

Devora's cheeks redden as she picks up the brush. "My penance?"

I nod and shuffle out of the way so Devora can stride forward and kneel before the second tombstone, the one beside Jax's. Two decades of weathering have reduced the names and dates carved into the stone to illegible scratches. She lifts the brush and scrubs, the red paint peeling away with each swipe of her powerful arm.

"Whose tombstone is this?" She eventually asks.

"The babies," I whisper. "We had five."

"Saen's beard, En. Five?"

"The midwife ordered us to stop trying after the fourth one, but…" I shrug, feeling very old on this hillside, staring at the stones marking the resting place of my family. "My domain is death. No life can ever come from this body."

"And the paint?"

"The villagers tolerated me because of Jax. They know what I am, and what I'm capable of, but he kept the peace. Now…" I shake my head.

Devora tosses the brush aside and rises in one fluid motion that reminds me she's a warrior, with all the quick reflexes and decisive gestures that implies. She draws a sheathed knife from under her cloak, placing it on Jax's headstone and stepping back like a supplicant with an offering.

Even encased in leather, the blade sings to me. I try to keep my voice steady. "You still have that old thing?"

"Of course I do. You asked me to keep it safe, so I did. And here it is, neglected, waiting to be called to service once again. You won't deny it one final chance for glory, will you?"

I can't stop staring at the dagger. "What are you asking?"

"Can you still sense the dead?"

"Always." The dead whisper in one voice, one clamoring jumble of sorrow and longing. I learned to ignore them long ago. Now that Jax has joined them, his voice is distinct, if I concentrate, but his desperation is the same, so I don't allow myself to listen.

"I can sense the living, too. You brought with you fifty men." I don't say that, with the dagger so close, their heartbeats pulse in my ears even at a distance of several miles.

"What about evil?"

I nod, tearing my eyes from the knife to look at my friend's face. "The air from the east has been laden with the scent of brine for a fortnight."

"Then you know why I'm here."

"I'm old enough to be a grandmother now." I hold up my brown, clawed hands. "I've spent the last thirty years farming, not monster hunting."

"I have fifty men with me, my fifty finest, and yet not one of them can hold a candle to you. Even my best men made their names fighting hellhounds and cultists, not Deep Lords. I can't ask a man who cut his teeth fighting puppies to go after the bitch who whelped them. I need *you*, En."

"Surely there are other retired hunters—"

"Those few who remain are living off their spoils on tropical islands somewhere, fat and useless. You and I are all that's left. We are all that stands between what exists now and a return to the time of the Deep Lords. Think of all the lives you'll save. Think of the glory. Think of the alternative!"

I stop and survey the land I've lived on for the last three decades, taking in the drafty farmhouse, the snow-covered fields, the lonely headstones. I look at my hands, so dark with sun and callused with labor. Somewhere inside me, I can feel the cold fire simmering in my gut, my power burning like glowing coals, longing to be put to use. The presence of the dagger is stoking a fire I've spent thirty years smothering.

"This battle will be our last one," I say. There's an acrid flavor on the back of my tongue that tastes faintly of leather and brass. "I can feel it."

"Do you want to die here, hated by your neighbors, alone and miserable? Or do you want to die on the battlefield, inspiring songs the bards will sing for centuries?"

Her words are like a spark to kindling. I grit my teeth against the pain, struggling to keep my internal fire controlled in my excitement. The voices of the dead are suddenly insistent, and above the din I can hear Jax; I can feel him urging me onward as if his hands were pressed against my shoulders.

Nodding, I lift the dagger from the headstone and draw it from the sheath. The runes coiled along the blade glow at my touch and my whole arm buzzes with the promise of the lives we'll take, the corpses we'll raise, the souls we'll summon to do our bidding.

I find myself smiling. "One final adventure."

## 2

My muscles have lost the memory of how to ride a horse, and the road is hard on my bones. After an afternoon on horseback I feel as if I'm about to shake apart into tiny splinters, as if my body is held together only by my leather armor, which has grown stiff with age and chafes me at every opportunity. Devora rides beside me with the practiced ease of someone who has spent most of her life wearing armor on horseback, only adding insult to my injury.

Ahead of us, fifty men ride. With my power no longer so closely reined, the soldiers stink of mortality, a thick, sweaty meat smell that churns my stomach. My vision is not what it used to be, but even in the hazy light of dusk I can see the soldiers periodically glancing back at me, their stares equal parts curiosity and judgment.

"What did you tell them about me?" I finally ask Devora.

"Only that you're the greatest necromancer in the Nine Worlds."

"Dev!"

"You can't say it's not true."

"Being the only necromancer is not the same as being the best."

"It is. And you're more powerful than ever you've been, so it's truer now than it ever was."

"Well then, the greatest necromancer in the Nine Worlds hasn't ridden a horse in years, and needs a respite."

"We're almost in Torren Vale, and can stop there for the night. There's a tavern there I think you might remember, in fact."

"The Suckling Pig, right? It was our favorite haunt. Isn't that where we picked up Jax?"

"You mean where he and I got into a fistfight and I knocked him flat? Yes."

I laugh. "Saen's beard, I'd nearly forgotten about that. The Pig was a squalorous pit, but it does have some good memories."

"It was *our* squalorous pit," Devora says, grinning.

Alas, when we leave Devora's men to make camp and go to The Suckling Pig well after sunset, it is nothing like we remember. The long tables and benches have been replaced with round tables and clusters of chairs, and the battle-scarred monster hunters laughing at bawdy jokes have been replaced by entire families making polite conversation. The bar is gone, and in its place stands a small shrine to Saen and a young musician strumming a lute for tips. Instead of the reek of stale beer and rancid sweat, the tavern is thick with the appetizing scent of roasted meat.

Conversation in the tavern stalls when we enter, all eyes watching us. My mouth is suddenly dry. "I don't think we belong here anymore."

Devora sighs. "It's like this all over the Nine Worlds. I had hoped this place would retain some of its original charm but... Ah, well. At least the food's probably better now."

We find a seat in the back corner. The other diners return to their meals, except for a few who make a hasty retreat.

"There was a time when we were celebrated, honored. Now people skulk away in fear instead of buying us drinks," I mutter.

"They don't know what it was like thirty years ago. They don't remember what we did for them."

"Not all of them have forgotten." I rise and go to the bard. I drop a coin into his basket and whisper a request in his ear. I return to my seat smiling.

"What did you do?" Devora asks.

The bard strums a familiar minor key on his lute and strikes up a tune. Devora lets out a bark of laughter after the first line, and the other diners shift in their seats, eyeing her as if she's a wild dog.

The bard, to his credit, never misses a beat, and his voice is clear and fine over the clink of dishes. When he gets to the chorus, Devora and I join in, because of course we know this song, better than any other.

*Monsters fall and Deep Lords cry*
*As the Maids of Death go by*
*Sword and dagger and sorcery*
*Beware the Maids of Death are nigh*

The second verse begins, and Devora calls for ale. A stout middle-aged woman in an apron marches over to us, scowling. Her cheeks are flushed and she's hiding one hand behind her back. "You're not welcome 'ere," she snarls.

"Excuse me?" Devora demands, rising to her full height and glaring down at the woman. The song abruptly stops as every pair of eyes in the dining room turns to us again. "This song is about us."

The barmaid lifts her chin. "I know exactly who y'are, and you're not welcome. Please go."

Devora clenches her jaw so hard I can hear her teeth grinding. Her hand goes to the pommel of her sword. I place my hand over hers and the touch of my cold fingers brings her attention to me.

"Our coin is as good as any other," I tell the barmaid.

The woman turns her crimson face to me. "You and your kind left this place a shambles after the Deep Lords fell, and I swore to me Da before 'e passed on that I'd never let that 'appen again. This 'ere is a nice, respectable place now, 'ardly the place for the likes of you."

"We rescued the Nine Worlds from eternal torment, and *this* is the thanks you offer us?" Devora bellows.

My fingers grip Devora's wrist hard. "She's right, Dev. Don't you remember the celebration? We destroyed this tavern after we took down Zahiel."

The remaining diners gasp.

I roll my eyes. "Zahiel. Zahiel, Zahiel. He's not coming back, so we can say his name all we like. He has no power on this plane anymore, we saw to that."

They're not listening. Mothers cover their children's ears and fathers round up their families to usher them out the door. The barmaid is apoplectic. "Get out, *now*."

Devora draws her sword, quick as lightning. The barmaid gives a strangled cry and staggers back, raising the cleaver clutched in her fist.

"Stop!" I shout. In that instant, I do what comes naturally. The room chills, my breath frosting in the air despite the fire in the hearth. "We don't harm innocent women," I tell Devora as the icy void inside me sucks the heat from her body, draining away her rage.

My friend lowers her sword. She turns to stare at me with a bemused expression. Her eyes, both seeing and unseeing, swivel to look at my fingers on her arm. She hisses and yanks her wrist from my grip; four long, finger-shaped burns discolor her skin, the marks black and limned with frost.

"We need to get out of here," I say.

Devora nods dumbly. Her skin is pale and her lips have taken on a blue tinge. I grasp her arm, careful to touch her sleeve and not bare flesh.

The barmaid watches us, still gripping her cleaver with such intensity her fingers are white and her hand shakes. A cook has emerged from the kitchen with a rolling pin, and the young bard remains perched on his stool by the shrine, holding very still, as if hoping to be forgotten.

I pause in the doorway. "I'm sorry we damaged your fine establishment. We thought we were invincible and that the Nine Worlds owed us a debt of gratitude."

The barmaid's reply quavers. "Seems like some of you still think that way."

Rage flares cold in my chest. My palm itches to hold the dagger sheathed on my arm and I imagine the barmaid's death. Her soul would taste like bitter hops and sweet cider. At the thought of carnage, my power boils like tar, threatening to bubble to the surface, threatening to make corpses of everyone in the room. How easy it would be to make them all regret their unkindness.

The woman's face grows slack with fear, and I know she can see the blue fire behind my eyes. I offer them all a sarcastic bow before making a quick exit with Devora in tow.

### 3

We return to the encampment to eat and sleep with the soldiers. Like riding, I haven't missed road rations or sleeping on the rocky ground.

Devora rubs absently at the burn on her arm when she thinks I'm not looking, but doesn't speak to me. She behaves as if nothing is amiss in front of her army, but I can sense the tension between us. Her men sense it too; I can tell from the wide berth they give her moving around the campsite, from their downcast eyes and the soft murmur of their collective voices. I miss the nervous laughter and excited energy of a monster hunting party's camp before the big battle. A pall hangs over us instead, exacerbated by the chill in the air.

I taste our deaths again, blood and sweat and brass commingled with turned soil and bitter roots.

～

In the morning, we ride out to the monster's lair. Our party is quiet, the only sounds the clink of armor and clop of hooves. We leave the horses at the village's outer edge and head in on foot, Devora and I leading the approach. For a moment it feels like old times; for a moment in the rush of anticipation I can forget my age, and Devora's strangeness, and the unseasoned men who follow us into battle.

The town of Draleton has been abandoned for some decades, probably since the time of the Deep Lords. Birds roost in the collapsed roofs of shops and homes alike. The streets are clogged with animal leavings and detritus. The air crackles with an unnatural silence, and the empty shop fronts echo with ghostly conversations and phantasmal laughter.

We arrive in the town square to find a chalk circle large enough to encompass the entire area drawn on the ground. The fountain in the center of the square, empty of water, is surrounded by candles melted down to the flagstones. The fountain itself is painted with dried blood and draped with rotting intestines, but it remains untouched by carrion beasts. Not even rats and vultures will eat sacrifice-tainted meat.

Silence falls as the rattling and creaking of armor ceases. Every man in the company stops at the edge of the circle, wary of the runes sketched on the ground.

I turn to Devora beside me. "It must be Bethor."

"Why do you say that?" Her expression is hard, as if she's speaking to a stranger.

"This is a summoning circle. If a Deep Lord is dead, there's nothing left to summon, and Bethor is the only one we never killed. He was banished back to the Deep instead, where I imagine he became king after we destroyed Zahiel."

"Couldn't it be a new evil?" Lightning flashes in her good eye and the runes on her armor flare to life like fireflies at twilight.

"Unlikely," I say, examining the runes on the circle. The scrawled writing tugs at my memory, as if familiar, but I can't place it. I step over the chalk symbols and approach the gory altar. "It would have to be summoned by someone who knew the Deep Lord's name and had some method of summoning, like a relic. A bone or a scale or…" I kneel and pick up a bloody tusk. "A tooth."

Devora draws her sword and turns to her men, raising the weapon above her head. She's glowing like the sun now, the white-hot electricity of Saen's blessing snapping and crackling around her like a saint's halo. "Did you hear that? Our foe is Bethor, a creature we've defeated before. That means we can defeat him again. For the safety and sanctity of the Nine Worlds, we *must* defeat him again. Who's with me?"

The soldiers raise their weapons and give enthusiastic cries of support. I'm surprised; only moments ago they acted as if they were marching to their deaths. But who could fail to be inspired by Devora's charisma, by her bravery?

Even if there is an edge of madness to it.

I wonder if that madness is new, or if I only have the perspective to see it now.

The reek of brine reaches my nostrils, so strong it makes me gag. Devora whirls as Bethor lurches into the town square. Like all the Deep Lords, Bethor looks as if he were pieced together by a child from a loose pile of mud and twigs and stones, only magnified a thousand times and given a terrible will for destruction.

He's even bigger than I remember, taller than the highest castle turret. His body is the same mad, jumbled shape that has haunted my nightmares for thirty years: too many limbs, too many eyes, an unspeakable number of mouths, floundering forward rather than walking, limbs flailing and eyes rolling, mouths grinning and snapping at the air. A pair of huge tentacles lash out from the center of his body, tipped with talons the size of swords. He opens all his mouths and roars, the sound deafening, and then all I can hear is ringing.

Devora leads the charge as her company surges forward. She shines like a glorious beacon, and for a moment I'm back in the old days, necromancy coursing through me, undead servants at my side. I can almost hear Jax screaming his war cry, bringing his sword down on the monster's neck in his signature strike.

Devora's men work as a unit, their experience showing in the intricately choreographed dance of battle. Archers loose a volley of arrows, and then a squad of spearmen launch their heavier missiles. When Bethor is bristling with weapons like a giant porcupine, they rush him with swords and axes, hacking and stabbing. They duck the swipes of his massive arms and the lashing of his deadly tentacles. For a moment, I think perhaps they might finish the battle before I've even had a chance to take part.

But then they begin to visibly tire. Fighting a Deep Lord is not like fighting an army. Armies suffer losses; men grow weary and retreat. Deep Lords grow only stronger with the heat of battle, and I've never once met a monster inclined to retreat, no matter how terrible his injuries.

Bethor kills three men with a swipe of one wicked talon. Their deaths jolt me from my inaction like a hard punch to my gut. I draw my dagger and cold fire burns down my arms and into my hands. Hearing my call, the dead soldiers rise again, stumbling forward to stab at the monster. He knocks them down and they rise once more, and again, until he grabs them each in turn and rips their arms from the sockets.

He turns to tackle the living soldiers who remain, but Devora is there, her sword hot and bright as if fresh from the blacksmith's forge. She severs one of Bethor's tentacles and thrusts the blade through the creature's body. He roars again, shaking the very earth, sending us all tumbling to our knees.

A blast of cold air brings sudden snowfall, dampening the sounds of combat and the stench of death.

Devora's sword is stuck fast in Bethor's center mass. He claws at the weapon with a dozen hands as black ichor pours from the wound, hissing as it strikes the flagstones. He thrashes and flails, his remaining barbed tentacle spinning through the air, scything through as many of our company as he can in his death throes. Finally he falls, and with one last gust of rotten breath, he dies.

In the quiet that follows I hear heavy breathing, grunting, someone moaning, someone else sobbing. Snow spins down and covers everything in a surreal layer of white. I'm not sure the extent of the carnage, but my power finds corpse after corpse after corpse. Each body feels like an empty vessel, a jar that's too light when lifted.

The souls of the freshly dead howl in my ears.

"Saen's beard, En. I didn't know you could raise corpses like that now," Devora gasps at me. She grins and claps me on the shoulder, not noticing my flinch away from her touch. "Used to be calling undead that sturdy took what, two days of summoning? Chalk circles and animal sacrifices and chanting and the whole bit."

"Did you do this?" I ask, gesturing at the bloody havoc before us.

"What are you going on about?"

The remainder of her company surrounds us. They're wounded, bloody, panting and dragging their swords. They're also angry, their rage washing over me in waves like lava pouring into the cool ocean. The heat of it makes me feel sick.

"I know the writing in the summoning circle, Dev. I'd recognize your chicken-scratch anywhere. And there's no one else who could have possessed Bethor's relic. It had to be you. You waited until Jax was dead—that's why I scented brine in the air not two days after his death. You didn't come to his funeral because you were busy summoning Bethor."

"How dare you!" Devora shouts, but the denial only makes the truth ring out. If it were a preposterous suggestion, she would have laughed.

"You thought we'd relive our glory days one last time," I say. My chest burns with sorrow, like there's an empty space in my heart sucking the marrow from my bones.

Devora's men heft their swords and axes and start toward her, their expressions grim.

She grits her teeth and brandishes her sword but it's not crackling with electricity anymore. Saen's blessings only apply to Deep Lords; he won't grant her special powers to harm men. Devora is a force of nature even on a bad day, but these are twenty of her best men and now she's only one warrior. One old, scarred warrior, blind in one eye, with no special powers.

My old friend looks at me with fear in her eyes for the first time in our long acquaintance.

# 4

The men move as one toward Devora, their bodies taut with menace. I should leave her to them and their bloody justice. I should let them avenge their fallen comrades.

But I can't.

When I exhale, the icy wind blasts us all. Frost forms on Devora's eyelashes and her teeth chatter. Snow spins down faster, creating drifts at our feet, covering the dead like a burial shroud.

And then the corpses rise, one by one, lifting their weapons and turning to face their living counterparts. It should frighten me how little effort I expend to raise so many, so freshly dead they're still warm, but it doesn't frighten me at all. It feels good, raising them, like I'm unclenching a muscle I haven't released in thirty years. I smile at the sensation of my power, finally truly unleashed, flowing through me as I've never allowed it to do. I feel like I'm finally myself, finally the person I'm meant to be.

A battle ensues, much of it obscured and muffled by the blizzard, but I don't need to see or hear to know the outcome. The dead fight fearlessly, beyond pain or consequences, and each time a living soldier falls I simply command him to rise again as part of my personal army.

Each death thrums through me, making me tingle, urging me on. In my hand, the dagger is at once hot as a brand and cold as an icicle. My power licks out, touching the corpse of the monster, and before I can wonder whether a Deep Lord can be raised as an undead creature, I've done it, jerking the corpse upright like a puppeteer with a marionette.

Bethor heaves himself to his many feet and towers over the combatants. His hundreds of eyes are blank and unseeing, his dozens of jaws hanging slack to reveal teeth like daggers, and his remaining tentacle lashes like the appendage of an angry cat. The sounds of combat cease as the living stare in awe. Someone takes Saen's name in vain, and then the few living soldiers who remain flee into the snow.

Devora approaches, her chest heaving, her brow slick with exertion, the heat radiating from her body melting the snow before it can touch her. She smells even more powerfully now of sweat and brass, and it churns my stomach. Her gaze flickers to the undead monster above us, and then back to me. "Grak, En. You're even more powerful than I thought."

The dagger pulses in my grip. "Do you remember why I gave up necromancy?"

She shrugs, watching Bethor warily. "You were in love with Jax."

"No. I gave up monster hunting for Jax, for the family he wanted to have. I gave up necromancy for another reason. Do you remember?"

She shakes her head. "No."

"I'm the only living necromancer because all the others were killed as children."

Devora blinks at me. "I know. What path are you attempting to lead me down?"

"Parents kill their own children if they show the signs, Dev. That's how much people fear this power." I hold up my hand, wreathed in blue fire. "Didn't you ever think there was a reason for that?"

"Power over life and death scares people—"

"No." I sigh. "It's not just that. Necromancy feeds on death.

And the strongest power comes from sacrifice. That's why sacrifice summons a Deep Lord, that's why it fans the flames of my power. What did you sacrifice to raise Bethor?"

She hesitates before answering. "A goat."

"The traditional sacrifice. But what would have been more powerful? What would have brought him here quicker, with all his faculties intact, as a god instead of merely a monster?"

Devora licks her lips. She glances around, her eyes practically spinning in their sockets as she looks for a way out. "A human sacrifice."

"And what is the most potent of all sacrifices?"

"Someone loved."

We stare at each other for a few seconds. The only sound is the soft hiss of snow falling.

Devora lunges at me, but Bethor's tentacle wraps around her before she can even heft her sword, holding her with the strength of rigor mortis. I step up to my old friend and show her my dagger one last time, runes gleaming along its polished surface. "Thank you for taking care of this for me. Being reunited with my blood-forged silver has been...indescribable. And I suppose I should thank you for summoning Bethor, too, and getting me into this whole mess." I reach up and lay my hand against Bethor's nearest snout. His skin is squamous and repulsive under my palm. "I never would have unleashed myself this way without your influence."

"I understand why you want to do this, En, I really do," Devora pleads. "But wouldn't it be better to have a companion to fight evil by your side than a sacrifice?"

"Saen's beard, Devora! Who are we going to fight? We killed the last Deep Lord. Our glory days are over. Can't you see?" I let my power flare bright like a bonfire. My eyes become pits of flame and my mouth a beacon of death. "I'm the mother of death. I *am* the thing the heroes fight; this is my destiny."

I slit her throat with my blade before she can say another

word. She writhes in Bethor's grip, her eyes bulging. Blood cascades down her torso to pool at her feet.

As she dies, my power surges, burning colder and brighter, the blizzard around us swirling into a maelstrom. I shudder and gasp, my whole body singing, my whole being crying out in ecstasy.

Devora goes limp. When I command her to rise, I think how pretty her lifeblood looks against the silver of her armor and hair, the white snow, her pale skin. It's an improvement, in the end.

Bethor's tentacle lifts me gently. He still smells of brine, but it's less offensive now that he's dead and covered in a layer of snow. Bearable, even.

"You wanted to relive our glory days, old friend," I tell Devora's walking corpse. "And so you shall."

# A LEGACY OF GHOSTS

I haven't seen my mom in the flesh for over a decade, but the exact moment she dies she appears to me. She materializes like condensation on a bathroom mirror, as if she's been waiting for this moment, hovering on the other side, anticipating the instant when the hospital would remove the tube from her lungs.

Of course, her ghost doesn't look like a 64-year-old woman in a wheelchair, skinny and ravaged by lung cancer, so for a second the pieces don't connect. I squint at a brunette in her thirties, wearing neon green leggings, an oversized sweater, and white Keds, like something out of a Van Halen music video. I can't see it, but I know with a sixth sense her teased ponytail is held in place with a scrunchy, probably a pink one.

My brain is just starting to recognize the mom of my childhood when she shouts, "HA! You *can* still see ghosts!"

I flinch. "You've been waiting a long time to say that."

"You bet your ass I have." She takes a drag on an ephemeral cigarette; my nose burns with the smoke of ghostly tobacco. "How do you get them to leave you alone?" She glances around, surprised, I guess, to find herself alone on the corporeal plane in my house. Her home would have been crowded with the dead, all clamoring for her attention, an endless parade of the desperate and damned.

I shiver, remembering cold hands plucking at my childhood pajamas. "They don't mess with me, and I don't mess with them."

She narrows her eyes.

My phone rings. I usually let it go to voicemail but I really, really need an excuse to stop talking to my mom, so I grab it and turn away from her ghost. She materializes in front of me again almost instantly and my lungs clench tight in my chest. "Hello?"

"Miss Huddle? My name is Candace. I'm a nurse at Mercy Hospital. Are you sitting down?"

"My mom is dead. Yes, thank you, I know. Anything else?"

"How—how do you…"

"You know what my mom did for a living?"

The nurse hesitates. "She was a psychic, right?"

"Yep. I inherited her gift. She's here with me now." My eyes flick to my mom, long legs pacing around my tiny kitchen, cigarette dangling precariously between two fingers. "She wants you to know she really appreciates all the care everyone at your hospital gave her. Thank you for calling."

Mom glares at me as I lower the phone. "Why'd you say that?"

I press my lips together to hold back a sharp reply: *Because caring for you was no picnic, and I'm glad I didn't have to do it.* Slipping into my teenage habits instead, I say only, "It was a nice thing to do for someone who lost a patient today."

Mom's nose wrinkles. "You were always so fucking nice. I see that hasn't changed."

*And you were always so fucking nasty; that hasn't changed, either.* "Thanks, Mom. I try." I offer her a sarcastic smile and go into the living room. I kneel at the altar against one wall and start pulling items from the drawers: a silver athame, a bowl made of bone, a silk cloth embroidered with runes, a candle made from human tallow.

"You don't do the work anymore, so why do you still have all that?" Mom asks. "Thinking about taking up the family business again now your competition is out of the way?"

"Something like that." I don't look at her. I drape the cloth over the altar, lay out the knife, go to the kitchen to fill the bowl with water. I light the candle and slit the tip of my pinky finger, letting my blood drop into the bowl. Then, I begin to chant the words, the words that will send my mother's ghost out of the corporeal plane, banishing her to the ethereal forever.

I've prepared for this spell for years. What I didn't prepare for was my mother.

Peals of hard-edged laughter fill the house. I cover my ears but her voice grinds into my head anyway. The reek of cigarette smoke fills my throat until I gag. The lights flicker and go out; the candle flame wavers and flares like a blast from a blowtorch, sending me reeling back from the altar.

Something cold rakes my back, something cold and sharp, like claws, like the fingernails of a dead woman.

"You haven't used your gift for a lifetime," my mother thunders, a lamp flying across the room to shatter against the wall. "You never let me finish teaching you everything you needed to know, and the most important lesson was that a medium only becomes more powerful in death."

The floor bucks violently, the house trembling as if I'm caught in a sudden earthquake. It sounds like a freight train bears down on the house, like an airplane is about to crash-land on the roof, like a herd of elephants stampedes across the yard. I want to do what I did as a child, curling into a little ball with my hands over my ears.

I remind myself: I'm not a child anymore. I force myself to my feet and snatch my purse from the hook by the door as I rush out of my own home. I run down the sidewalk and throw myself into my car, starting the engine and backing out of the driveway.

I pause in the street to look back at my house. Even with the car windows up and the motor running, I hear crashing sounds, the blare of a TV or radio—maybe both—turned to maximum volume. The lights in the windows flicker and flash. The front door opens and slams shut. Rage claws its way up my throat and exits my mouth in a long, low wail. She's destroying my home, my carefully constructed safe space, purely out of spite. Again, I fight the urge to shut down, swallowing my sobs.

It's time to go to Plan B.

Danielle greets me with open arms when I arrive on her doorstep. Her dark hair is streaked with gray and her eyes are surrounded by crow's feet, but otherwise she looks much as she always has. She smells of sage and sandalwood as we embrace, and memories assault me, memories of my teenage years, spent hiding out at Danielle's new age shop when home became particularly unbearable. I can almost feel her well-worn tarot cards under my fingers, taste the peppermint tea she always made to soothe my nerves, hear the tinkle of bells on the front door as customers entered and exited the shop.

Of course, the shop is long gone—now Danielle sells the same mystical items online, from the comfort of her own home. She invites me in, past a dining room stacked with boxes and bags of inventory, and I say hello to the big black tomcat, Merlin, her familiar and pet. I'm amazed Merlin is still alive—he must be more than twenty years old—but I don't say so, not in front of him.

The murmur of muffled voices reaches me, and I glance at Danielle.

"Coven is on the back patio," Danielle says, and my eyes again well with tears, but this time they're tears of gratitude.

Twelve women are gathered under the tin roof of Danielle's patio, their faces dimly lit by citronella candles. A few I remember from my time in the shop, regular customers, but the rest are new. Most smile at me but a few frown and look away.

Danielle steps onto the patio and places her arm around my shoulders. "This is Morgan, everyone." She turns to me and whispers, "Not everyone agreed with the vote, but they'll still help."

Someone drawls, "The tyranny of the majority."

Others sigh or chortle, and the woman nearest me rolls her eyes. She stands, and she's well over six feet tall. Her voice is surprisingly deep and sonorous. "Welcome, Morgan. We're happy to help you, if we can. I'm Jessica."

I shake Jessica's long-fingered hand. She has a firm grip and looks me directly in the eyes, and I appreciate both. I take comfort from her confidence. There's something familiar about her, but I can't quite place where I know the planes of her face and the bright amber of her eyes.

Jessica smirks. "We had classes together in high school. I was called Evan, then."

I nod, remembering a quiet, shy young man I never really got to know. A far cry from the woman standing before me, whose charisma seemed to take up the whole patio, a radiant Amazon. "You look better as a blonde."

Jessica laughs, a loud bark too goofy to be fake. Her smile broadens and her posture relaxes. Her eyes go from amber to gold as her expression softens.

Danielle clears her throat, bringing me back to the patio, with its cloud of citronella and cigarette smoke, and the assembled witches watching me intently.

I turn to the coven. "Right. I really appreciate all your help. We don't have any time to waste. Mom's weakened by her earlier outburst at my house but she'll regain her strength quickly. Best to banish her while she's not at full strength."

Jessica nods and grins. "I've never banished a ghost before. It's exciting."

The rest of the group seems less enthusiastic. One woman stubs out her cigarette and shakes her head.

"I know this is asking a lot for someone most of you barely know. I can't thank you enough," I say.

"Just remember that the next time we call you with a favor," another woman says.

I nod, agreeing to this price. I would agree to a lot more, to rid myself of my mother's ghost permanently, but they don't need to know that. Merlin watches me from the window, blinking his big, round eyes, two glowing green lanterns in the dusky light.

As one, the group rises and goes into the yard. They've already placed their brooms in a circle and I step into it. Danielle pours salt around the circle, an added precaution. The wind stirs the trees ringing Danielle's backyard, pushing the swing on her ancient swing set so it issues a rusty squeak, tugging at my hair like the icy fingers of the dead.

Someone lights a candle and the flame is passed around the circle. With each woman holding a candle, it looks like I'm surrounded by glowing, disembodied heads. The night beyond each woman seems endlessly dark and cold, the stars and moon overhead blotted out by clouds. When everyone has quieted, Jessica raises her candle and calls to Hecate for her help. Jessica's voice is powerful and dramatic, and I can understand why they chose her for this part of the ritual. The neighbors are miles away and they can probably hear her appeal; surely the gods themselves can't ignore us.

Danielle begins the chant of the same words I used in my banishing ritual, a jumble of Gaelic and Latin, a few Germanic words thrown in for good measure. Like all magical language, it has power because we lend it meaning. The words themselves could be the ingredients from the back of a cereal box, but thirteen women reciting them as a mantra while focusing their will can make them into a powerful spell.

I just hope thirteen women will be enough.

The other women pick up the chant and it rises in volume and speed, the words crawling across my skin and making my hair stand on end. Danielle was true to her word: even the reluctant members of her coven chant with purpose and intensity. The air crackles with magical energy.

I stand in the circle for what feels like eternity, the wind whipping my hair into a tangled mess. The candle flames waver and flicker and a few have to be relit. The coven's voices rise and fall, the chant becoming a pulse that batters the inside of my skull. The minutes slouch into hours. Where is my mother's ghost? Did she drive herself into such a frenzy at my house that she effectively banished herself? My instincts say, no. I have to wait. Patience has never been a virtue of mine, and I fight the urge to check my watch for the time. The women in the circle sway with boredom. My legs ache. I'm ready to give up and start brainstorming a Plan C.

And then the barometric pressure drops so fast I feel it in my head, my belly, like I'm in an elevator that made an abrupt stop. I lean forward, suddenly nauseous with dread, a feeling I haven't missed since I mastered my ability to channel spirits twenty years ago. Behind the women in the circle, faces appear in the darkness, gray and drawn, eyes bright with hunger like silver coins. The faces of the dead.

Surprise and fear ripple around the circle as the women notice the visitors. Danielle continues chanting, raising her voice insistently until the other women rejoin the mantra, but their voices are tentative now, and even Danielle's hands tremble holding their candle. Her eyes meet mine, communicating a silent plea: *Hurry.*

"You can't rush the dead, honey." Mom materializes inside the circle, leaning over to speak in Danielle's face. She glows with unearthly, ephemeral light. She looks, now, how she looked on her television show: a forty-something woman in a blue skirt-suit, her bottle-blonde hair expertly styled into a French twist.

"This is how you want to be remembered?" I ask, filling my

voice with contempt, hoping to draw her attention away from Danielle.

When she turns to me, her face is so coated with pancake makeup it looks blurred, soft-focus, wrinkles smoothed over and age spots concealed. Beautiful.... but also plastic, fake, like a genuine smile would crack her face in half. She chuckles, sauntering over to me on heels that never sink in the grass. "Why wouldn't I want to look like this? I was one of *People* Magazine's most beautiful people in this outfit."

"Thanks to a team of stylists and speech writers and marketing experts. You look like President Barbie."

The cigarette appears again between her fingers and she takes a long drag, ghostly smoke expelling from her nostrils as she talks. With her eyes glowing and smoke wreathing her head she reminds me of a dragon. "You never approved of what I did with the gift. I can't help it if you rejected your legacy, but why does that have to apply to me?" She flicks the cigarette away and it cartwheels through the air, a slim, glowing white stick with a burning red tip. The coven watches as it lands on one woman's chest. I think her name is Lorraine? I remember her from Danielle's shop. Back then she was the type who never deviated from the pagan uniform of broomstick skirts, loose blouses, and velvet kimonos, and she hasn't changed in that respect in twenty years.

There's an instant of silence and hesitation where we hold our collective breath.

Lorraine screams and brushes the apparition from her shirt. It evaporates in the air but leaves behind a scorch mark in her blouse and a small, round burn on the revealed flesh of her sternum. Danielle shouts at them to stay and hold the circle, but two other women hustle Lorraine, still shrieking, out of the yard and into the house, and then we're down from thirteen to ten— eleven, if you count me. I'm going to have to count for double, I guess.

Mom laughs, the sound like rusty chains dragging on rough

asphalt. "If that's all it takes to scare off your pathetic wannabe-witches, Danielle, this is gonna be easier than I thought."

"Hold the circle!" Danielle barks. She takes up the chant again. The remaining women close in, filling in the gaps, bringing the circle tighter. Their chanting is louder now, more urgent, the words tripping over one another. I close my eyes and let the magic wash over me, an ocean of electricity where I can float.

Mom's power is a hot slap ripping me from the cool tide. When I open my eyes, the other women have been knocked to the ground. Shouting in panic, they scramble to their feet and run for the house. All except Danielle and Jessica.

Now we're down from thirteen to three.

I step out of the circle and grab a broom. The three of us close in around Mom, chanting. Danielle has always been powerful, and Jessica's formidable magic crackles from her aura like a raging bonfire, and then there's me.

Mom laughs again, even as the circle shrinks around her, barely wider than her ghostly hips. Her eyes are the burning red cherries of her cigarettes. Behind her, the hungry dead surround us, pressing in, wearing expressions of pain and longing. They whisper in my ears, a susurrus of misery, and over it all, my mother's voice: "You'll never beat me. You came from me, you're a fraction of me and my power. You should really give up before someone else gets hurt, Morgan."

Under the reek of cigarette smoke, the air smells like ozone, like a summer storm, like lightning about to strike. My gut clenches tight, threatening to make me expel everything I've eaten today.

"Stop holding back," Jessica interrupts the chant to shout at me. Her eyes glow like twin suns. Danielle squeezes my hand, nodding agreement, never breaking the chant. Her hair is bright white flame and her voice is impossibly loud, the chanting of multitudes issuing from one mouth.

I shake my head, trying to communicate that this is it. This is all I have. Mom is right; I've never been as powerful as she is, and I never will be. I gave up magic a long time ago, and with it I gave up the ability to free myself of my mother's ghost. Despair sinks inside me like a lead weight.

"She'll never be able to match me," Mom bellows. The wind tears at us, a cold blast laden with the stench of brimstone and nicotine. The dead howl around us, a ravenous maelstrom, ragged fingers tearing at our hair, our clothes, our skin. The creaking swing issues a rusty scream as it tears away from the swing set and disappears over the roof of the house. Tree branches crack and tumble to the ground all around us.

"You betrayed me, Danielle, right up until the end." Mom rears back, the size of a skyscraper, a mountain, a massive churning tsunami. I scream Danielle's name, but it's too late. Mom's ghost crashes over Danielle, and the last thing I see is Danielle looking at me, opening her mouth as if to say one last desperate word, and then we're all engulfed in darkness.

I come up from the darkness and I'm surrounded by bodies, too many of them, none giving me air. The faces are wan, their fingers touching me are cold, and their voices pleading with me are soft and despairing. Their eyes shine like pearl buttons. Am I in the afterlife? Have I crossed over?

I push the apparitions away, both physically and psychically, so I can get my bearings. I'm not sure what happened to my shoes, but there is grass tickling the soles of my bare feet. When I stand, the ground is solid beneath me. The breeze ruffles my hair. I breathe a sigh of relief; not dead.

As the spirits step back, Danielle's collapsed form is revealed. My stomach drops and I run to her. My fingers pressing at her neck can't find a pulse. Her skin is already going cold.

A hand on my shoulder makes me look up. Jessica looms above me. "We have to finish this."

Mom's ghost is gone, probably too weak to stay corporeal. The other ghosts swirl around us, moaning and weeping and gnashing their teeth. It's hard to think with all the uproar.

"I can't do it," I whisper.

"What?" Jessica grabs my arm and hauls me to my feet. "Danielle just died for this."

"I don't think I'm strong enough, even with your help." I can't look Jessica in the eyes. Tears sting my cheeks.

"Then call Danielle from the other side."

I shake my head and step back from her. "You don't know what you're asking."

"Why not? Danielle would give anything for you."

I sigh. I've never told anyone this, except Danielle. "Being a medium isn't what you think. I quit because the ghosts were being called from the other side to talk to their loved ones and then they couldn't get back. They become the hungry dead." I nod to the twisted, desperate, gray faces that surround us, their moans rising briefly with the recognition. "Mom was using the ghosts for financial gain, then leaving them to wander the corporeal plane for eternity."

"So, if we called Danielle from the other side…."

"She'd be doomed to the same fate. I can't do that to her." A sob chokes me. "Danielle was like a mother to me when mine didn't want me anymore."

"And that's why your mom is haunting you. Because you didn't want to scam families out of money to torture their dead loved ones."

"When I rejected my gift she took it personally. We haven't talked for more than twenty years. She's waited a long time to be able to punish me."

Jessica nods. "A tale as old as time."

That startles a laugh from me. "Sure."

Jessica finds two candles on the ground and fishes in the pocket of her denim skirt for matches. "No, really. I'm a therapist in my day job. Most of my clients are people who

couldn't live up to a parents' expectations—or didn't want to."
Jessica hands me a candle, lights a match, lets the wick catch,
and then uses the match to light her own candle. The air fills
with the scent of sulfur and wax burning. "You know Danielle
talked about you a lot."

I meet her eyes in the soft, golden candlelight. She's so
pretty, my stomach does a flip. "She did?"

"You were like a daughter to her. She was so proud of you
for making a life for yourself, getting past your mother's abuse."

I sniffle. "It wasn't abuse. She just disapproved of me."

One of Jessica's eyebrows arches. "You don't think this," she
waves her hand to encompass the dark backyard, the sighing
ghosts lingering in the shadows, Danielle's body cold on the
ground, "is abusive?"

"I guess I never really thought about it that way before. I
think she got angrier as she got older, too. She wasn't like this
when I was young."

"Stop making excuses for her and listen—I don't think we
have much time before she comes back, and we need to be
ready."

I shake my head. "Thank you, Jessica, really, but I can't risk
your life, too." I start toward the house, where a few fearful
witches watch us from the dark kitchen window. "I should go
home."

Jessica catches my arm in a firm grip. "This is your home.
Danielle's house and her coven will always be your home."

"I can't ask anyone else to die for me." I pull my arm from
her grasp and turn away from her.

"Danielle believed in you, Morgan, and she believed you
aren't a psychic medium at all."

The wind is picking up again, and the hungry dead are
growing louder, more raucous. "I can hear the dead right now,
Jessica. Even when they're on the ethereal plane, I can hear them.
All the time. They never shut up."

"But you were able to live a life anyway. How? How did you control your power?"

"I made them leave me alone!" The wind tugs at my hair. The ghosts issue a collective, panicked wail, and my ears pop, as if I'm on an airplane descending from cruising altitude. "She's back." Now it's my turn to grab Jessica's arm and pull her toward the house. "You should get inside."

Jessica fights me, and she's taller, stronger, has more leverage. She has to shout to be heard over the screaming ghosts, the tearing wind. "How did you control your power?"

"I bluffed, okay? I told them not to come near me or I'd send them all to Hell!"

Mom's ghost pops into existence beside me, blowing a cloud of cigarette smoke into my face. "Sadly for you, Hell doesn't scare me."

Jessica shouts, "Morgan, don't you get it? They *listened* to you."

Mom's eyes slide to Jessica. She raises her hand and flicks her wrist, like she's swatting an annoying fly, and Jessica hits the ground, so hard the air is knocked from her lungs and she lays there, flailing and gasping for breath.

"You ready to go home now?" Mom's gaze returns to me.

"Why do you want to spend your afterlife haunting me?" I ask, watching Jessica out of the corner of my eye.

Mom laughs, a throaty, malicious sound, and takes another drag on the cigarette. "You need my help, Morgan. Your life would be so much better if you would just accept your gift and use it."

I'm left speechless for a second, and then I manage to stutter, "I don't need you. I got by just fine without you for twenty years."

"Oh please. You live in a one-bedroom apartment and you work in a call center. No husband, no children. No legacy. You always needed me to guide you and tell you what to do. My only mistake was letting you move away from me and thinking maybe you could make it on your own, without your family."

The dead scream now, so loudly I can barely hear Mom's words over their shrieking. "Danielle was my family, and you killed her."

She flashes me that bright television smile that charmed millions of viewers all over the world for nearly a decade. "No, *you* killed her. All you had to do was cooperate. But you had to fight me—you always had to fight me. I'm your mother. I know what's best for you."

On the ground, Jessica sits up at last, sucking in deep breaths. Relief washes over me, and I realize just how afraid I was that she might die, too. She meets my eyes, trying to communicate something to me. An instant later she's invisible, the dead crowding in around me to shout in my ears, blocking her from view.

Mom keeps talking. "The first thing we'll do when we get back to your place is call the network. If you lose a few pounds there are no flaws makeup can't cover."

My hands go to my ears, trying to block out Mom's voice, trying to block out the chattering, wailing ghosts, but of course it doesn't work. Panic rises in me. What was Jessica trying to tell me? I'm not a medium. The dead listen to me. Those two things couldn't coexist. So, which was it? Why did it matter? I wish everyone would just shut up so I can think for a second.

"GET BACK, GET BACK, GET AWAY FROM ME." The words erupt from my mouth, deeper and louder than I've probably ever spoken. The other ghosts whirl away from me, their voices quieting, and even Mom takes one step back, a hand fluttering to her chest dramatically.

Jessica stands, dead leaves crunching under her shoes, and I can hear her footsteps, it's so quiet. My own frantic breathing is loud in my own ears. From the house, I can hear the concerned murmuring of the witches watching us through the window.

My eyes go to Danielle's limp form. What had she figured out that I didn't know?

"The ghosts listen to me," I say to Jessica.

She nods, once, and a smile curves her lips.

Revelation crashes over me. I turn to my mother. "The ghosts listen to me. The ghosts *never* listened to you."

"Of course they did," Mom says. "I summoned thousands—"

"Sure, you summoned them, but you could never send them back."

She snorts, affecting a casual pose. "And you think you can?"

I study her face. There's a flicker of fear there, a crack in her confidence. "I do, yeah. I think I can. I can send them all back across the veil, and I can send you there, too. Because I'm more powerful than you are, and I always have been." My heart is thumping hard now, but it's not with panic. I'm excited. "That's why you were always trying to control me, and put me down, and make me feel small. Your gift was everything to you, and you couldn't stand the thought of being surpassed by your own daughter."

She sniffs. "Don't be ridiculous."

I glance around me at the ghosts. They're still and silent, but their expressions aren't fearful or angry or even hungry anymore. Their gleaming eyes are brimming with hope.

They want me to send them back. They're waiting for it, and they've been waiting for a long time.

I take a deep breath, and I recite the banishing spell. I don't need to chant it as a mantra, or even say it more than once. The words are merely a focus for my will, and my will alone is enough to rip a hole between worlds, a jagged tear with its own gravity that threatens to suck me into it. I dig my heels into the earth as it starts to pull the ghosts into the brightness beyond. I flail, grabbing for something solid to hang onto.

Jessica's strong hands close around my waist.

We watch as the ghosts disappear into the light like water

swirling down the bath drain. Mom is the last to go, her hands reaching for me, clawing, desperate. She doesn't want to go, and it's because she's afraid. She's afraid to confront the souls of those she wronged on the other side—and she's afraid to leave me, afraid of what I'll become, or what I won't become, perhaps. She's terrified to leave her legacy in my hands, the hands of someone she's never understood, never accepted, and never really liked.

"It's okay, Mom. I'll be okay," I tell her. She screams something unintelligible as the vortex sucks her into it, and then she's gone.

I need a focus to close the portal, and my exhausted mind can't think of anything but the birthday song. After the first few words, Jessica joins in, her voice lending strength to mine. The tear in reality mends itself closed and Danielle's backyard is her backyard once again. Toads croak in the pond nearby, and crickets chirp in the grass at our feet. The last notes of the song fade away and the breeze ruffles my hair softly, without insistence.

I can breathe—really breathe—for maybe the first time in my entire life.

Jessica's RV always smells like sandalwood and sage—like home —no matter where we find ourselves. A photograph of Danielle graces the wall beside the kitchen, which is also the living room and the dining room, and sometimes also the game room or the nooky room when we're feeling amorous. Jessica is making beans on toast with just a sprinkle of cheese, my favorite breakfast, and I'm tracing a route to the next town on the map, when Merlin gives that peculiar chirp he only does when company's arriving. He hops down from the seat beside me and retreats into the bedroom just as the knock sounds at the door.

The woman standing outside looks like she's had a hard life.

Her skin is deeply lined in the way of heavy smokers, and for an instant my nose fills with the reek of my mother's cigarettes. "Can I help you?"

"I heard you're some kind of a psychic." She gets right to the point in the way of the desperate.

"Sorry," I say with a shrug. "You were misinformed. I'm not a psychic. I can't read your tarot or help you talk to your loved ones who crossed over."

"But Cheryl Stokes across the lake said you got her brother's ghost to stop haunting her. For free."

I smile. "I did. That's kind of what we do."

The woman blinks at me. "Look, I think something's haunting me, too. Are you a psychic or not?"

I nod, gesturing for her to come into the RV, eyeing the restless ghost that lingers behind her. "I can help with the haunting. But I'm not a psychic or a medium."

"Then what are you?"

From the kitchen, Jessica says, "She's a necromancer. Do you want butter or jam with your toast?"

# THE MOON IN HER EYES

Night in the forest is dense and close and smells of green things growing and the creep of shadows. My thoughts are consumed with the rabbit I'm hunting when I catch the scent of sunshine and peppermints. I pull up short, letting my prey scamper off into the ferns. I raise my head and breathe deep: sunshine and peppermints and the warm vanilla smell of human skin. My fur prickles and my hackles raise. There's a human in my woods.

I find her easily enough. She's not yet a teenager, just on the cusp of puberty, and she huddles in the hollow beneath an oak tree—*my* hollow in *my* oak tree—and shivers so violently I can hear her teeth clicking. A twig snaps beneath my paw as I approach and her breath catches. The scent of adrenaline rolls off her skin, hot and tangy. She's afraid, and rightfully so. I might be old and blind but these are still my woods. I am still a wolf.

We're near the border of my territory, here, closer than I generally like to be. Not a hundred yards from the hollowed oak, the trees and ferns give way to the velvety grass of neatly trimmed lawns. There's a loud bang, the sound of a screen door slamming, followed by heavy footsteps. I crouch defensively and the girl whimpers. The footsteps make their way across the nearest yard and crunch into the dead leaves at the edge of the forest. The combined odors of skunky beer and human sweat reach me and curl my lip.

"Hannah?" The man calls in a voice deep and gravelly. "Where you at? It's not safe in the woods alone at night, girl. Don't be stupid."

The girl holds her breath. She's silent as a rabbit hiding in a thicket.

The man calls for her a few more times, belches, scratches himself. "Fine, then, stupid brat. Stay out here all night for all I care." He turns and goes back to the house, his footsteps stumbling a little in the darkness, tripping on the porch steps and cursing, slamming the screen door.

The girl breathes again. She shifts in the hollow, scuffling her feet against the leaves, curling up into a ball. She sniffles and whimpers for a short time. Eventually her breathing slows as she falls asleep.

I hide myself a few yards from the oak and spend my night crouched among the ferns. When I wake at first light, the girl is gone.

My belly pinched with hunger, I find the clothes I keep stashed in a trash bag buried in a shallow grave. I go into civilization with my cardboard sign in one hand and an old coffee cup in the other, camping out in front of the strip mall on the edge of town. Enforcement of anti-panhandling laws here is lax and the landlord is sympathetic to my plight. Most people ignore me or drop a few coins into my cup. A few mutter about calling the cops. A man who smells like freshly mowed grass brings me a cup of coffee and a breakfast sandwich wrapped in crisp paper. The food tastes like chemicals, like metal machines and rubber-gloved hands, but I eat it anyway.

Once upon a time I was too proud to beg, and too proud to

eat food I hadn't caught myself. Those times are long past, eroded along with the forest, developed into housing complexes and apartment buildings. Game is sparse now, limited mainly to small birds and fat squirrels and the occasional rabbit. I have to supplement my diet somehow, and my self-respect is not so low that I'll stoop to dumpster-diving quite yet.

You might wonder why I don't attack the humans who invade my territory if I'm so desperate for fresh meat. Don't flatter yourselves. Humans like to think they're some kind of delicacy, but if you are what you eat, your kind are made of sugary drinks and preservatives and the inedible parts of animals rendered with chemicals and pressed into entertaining shapes. I'd rather eat garbage.

It's much easier to eat on your dime than it is to gnaw on your bones. By lunchtime I've collected a fair bit of change and I'm thinking about hitting up the sandwich place across the street with whatever I have. Then the scent of sunshine and peppermints hits me and I'm frozen in place. Multiple footsteps approach: two people; no, three. The girl is accompanied by the man—even under the liberal application of pine-scented aftershave I can detect the odors of sweat and beer oozing from his pores. There's a woman with them, also, a woman who is so quiet her footsteps barely register under the footsteps of the other two. She smells faintly of lavender, but otherwise she's invisible to my senses.

The man growls something about lazy beggars. My skin prickles, rage tingling behind my breastbone.

"Why does she have the moon in her eyes?" The girl asks. She thinks she's whispering low enough for me not to hear her, but of course I'm blessed with the hearing of the blind and also the hearing of the wolf.

"She has cataracts," the woman replies. Her voice is small and soft. "Remember, your Nana Drummond had them? She got an operation to have them removed before they were very bad."

"She should've taken care of them before they were irreversible," the man says, not bothering to lower his voice. Now that he's closer I can smell the cancer on his breath. He doesn't smoke anymore, but he did, for too long, and his death is closer than he realizes.

The scent of peppermints grows stronger as the girl approaches me. "Hello," she says.

I blink at her in surprise.

"Hannah, get back here," the man orders.

"I want to give her money," Hannah says, and I can picture her chin jutting out defiantly.

"Not my money, you're not."

I know that tone: it's a warning of impending violence. I should walk away, and fast, but I find myself rooted in place.

"It's not your money," Hannah says. "It's my money. I earned it walking dogs, and I can spend it on whatever I want."

"Clark, let her do something nice with it if that's what she wants," the woman says in her small voice. "She's trying to do something good."

"Shut up, Barb. She's trying to do something *stupid*."

With the quiet shuffle of old, soft paper, Hannah drops bills into my cup. I don't know how many, but it's probably ten or twenty dollars, depending on the value of the bills. "I'm sorry you have to beg for money. I hope this helps," she says in a whisper.

I nod and muster a smile. It feels unfamiliar and strange.

Clark is on top of us in a rush of heat and swearing. He pulls Hannah away from me. She screams, short and shrill, calling for her mother and stumbling down the sidewalk toward Barb. I snatch the bills from the cup and shove them in my pocket. Clark grabs my arm.

"Give that back."

I bare my teeth and snarl at him. I can't see his face but I can feel how his body reacts to the sound, tensing with fear, releasing endorphins, preparing to fight or flee.

The bells on the nearby restaurant door jingle and the peppermint and lavender odors retreat in a rush of hamburger-scented air.

"You're crazy. You're not even worth it," Clark says through gritted teeth. His breath on my face is rank.

I realize then we're gathering a crowd of onlookers. Not many, but a few. They keep their distance but they're obviously concerned. Even without vision I can sense their alertness, the tense posture of their bodies and the quickness of their breathing. "Hey man," someone says. "Let go of her. She's just an old lady. She's *blind*, man."

No one approaches, but Clark isn't stupid. Violent, dangerous, but not stupid. He's not going to hit an old woman in public in front of witnesses. I suspect he only hits his wife and daughter when he's sure nobody else is around. What a big, tough man he is, so unafraid to hit a defenseless woman.

Of course, I'm not defenseless. I'm just as dangerous as he is, even without a wolf's powerful jaws. I drop my cardboard sign and my hand finds the knife in my pocket, the one I've carried for years, because I'm not stupid, either. As Clark lets go of my arm and steps away from me, however, I find myself glad I don't have to use it.

"Don't let me see you here again," he says over his shoulder as he strides away.

Once his pine-beer stink has retreated, the onlookers retreat as well. Someone presses a wad of bills into my hand, murmuring something polite. I wait until I'm alone before slinking back into the forest.

My clothes once again buried, I shed my human guise to become a creature of fangs and fur. There was a time when the wolf-pelt was the one that felt like a disguise, but that was long ago, before I became a full-time resident of the forest.

I catch a chipmunk and gobble it down, fur and bones and all, barely tasting it. Then I nap for a while in the ferns near Hannah's house. I wake licking my chops, roused by the delectable odor of charred meat. I'm up and moving toward the scent before I'm even fully conscious. I know it's evening by the temperature, the fern fronds chilly as they brush my flanks.

Halting at the edge of the forest, I crouch in the dead leaves and listen. Clark mans the grill. He's drunk, the reek of bourbon searing my whiskers. He gives commands to Barb and Hannah, who obey with alacrity, stinking of fear.

Hannah doesn't bring him the bratwurst quickly enough and he swats her. She hits the ground. A growl burbles up in my throat and I swallow it. Hannah flees for the house and Clark follows, bellowing. The grill is unguarded while he screams at his wife and daughter in the kitchen. There's a sound of something crashing, Barb's voice, the thump of footsteps.

I make for the grill, pulling a bratwurst off the heat and swallowing it in one bite. I snatch another one and run for the trees, where I take my time enjoying it. When I'm done, Clark is still in the house, though I can't hear any fighting. The grill still smells like meat: steak, specifically. My favorite, and no doubt intended for Clark.

I'm full, two bratwurst more than enough food for my starved belly, but I can't resist the temptation. I run to the grill and grab the steak in my jaws. My mouth fills with hot, delicious beef flavor.

The screen door slams and I freeze. Someone gasps, and I can tell by the timbre of the voice that it's Hannah. Her breathing is rapid, staccato, her heartbeat hammering. She's probably never seen a wolf up this close before, with only a few feet of lawn separating us, no fence or wall or pit to keep her safe from the predator.

On those rare occasions that humans see my wolf, it always feels wrong, like a forbidden secret revealed, like the most intimate part of me exposed. Hannah doesn't move or speak for long, breathless seconds, as if she, too, realizes the gravity of the moment.

Then Hannah licks her lips and whispers something. I don't hear it the first time over the rush of blood in my own ears, but then she clears her throat and says it louder.

"Take it."

Clutching the steak in my jaws, I dip my head in acknowledgement and then make for the forest at a trot.

Hannah visits the forest again in the wee hours. She huddles in the hollow oak for a long time, sobbing, before she finally calms and falls asleep. I wait near the tree all night. I'm the only predator in these woods, but that doesn't mean the girl's safe. Clark doesn't chase after her this time, however, and in the morning she trundles back to the house.

I spend my day napping and eating chipmunks. That evening, Clark grills steak again, but this time he sits in a lawn chair near the grill, the delicate fabric and metal frame of the chair creaking under his weight. He swigs bourbon directly from the bottle. The combined scents of metal, oil, and gunpowder tell me there's a firearm in his lap, so I don't attempt to steal any meat, though my mouth waters. He eats the steak in his chair instead of going inside, as if taunting me.

Thunder grumbles as dusk settles over the neighborhood. Clark closes the grill and goes inside as the first fat raindrops fall. I retreat to the hollow oak and drift asleep to the patter of rain on the ferns.

The scent of peppermints, sunshine, and vanilla wakes me. A hand touches my fur. Hannah lets out a startled scream and backs away from the hollow, slipping on the wet earth and sliding to the ground.

I follow her out into the rain. She struggles to rise in the dark and the mud, sobbing and shrieking. Even with rain pounding down around us, her noises will attract attention if she doesn't hush.

Giving up the last scrap of my dignity, I approach her and lick her face like a dog.

Hannah screams, but then quiets. I can feel her staring at me, so I let my tongue loll from my mouth. I'd try to make puppy dog eyes at her, but that's difficult to do in the dark, with lenses blinded by a milky white film. After a few moments I lower myself back to the ground and nudge her hand with my snout. She makes a perplexed sound but strokes my wet fur.

I move toward the hollow and she follows, sniffling all the way. Together we climb beneath the oak and together we huddle against each other for warmth. Hannah shivers for many minutes, her teeth chattering, but eventually her trembling subsides. She curls up beside me and falls asleep, her fingers tangled in my fur.

Sometime during the night, the thunderstorm moves on. The sound of falling water is replaced by the chirping of crickets and the soft rustle of bat wings overhead. The forest's usual sounds are interrupted by booted footsteps and rasping breaths. I lift my head and scent the air: Clark is here, with his stink of alcohol and charred meat and cancer.

Hannah stirs beside me. She sucks in a breath as if she's about to speak, but then she hears the footsteps, the careless crash of boots on broken branches. She gasps and throws her arms around my neck, engulfing me in warm vanilla.

Clark stumbles toward the oak. I crouch low, a growl rolling in my chest.

"Hannah!" He shouts, his speech slurred. "Come out this minute. Your mother 'sworried 'bout you."

Hannah's fingers clutch at my fur reflexively, little pinpricks of pain blossoming on my skin where she tugs the strands. She buries her face in my side.

I catch a whiff of the gun, then. The fresh gunpowder is like pepper on the back of my tongue, acrid and burning.

"Hannah," he calls again. He staggers away from the tree.

"Clark, come back inside." A high, quavering voice and the scent of lavender.

Hannah's fingers release me and she starts for the mouth of the hollow. I move to block her with my body.

"It's late and it's dark," Barb reasons. "Come inside before it starts raining again."

"I told you to wait in the house," Clark snarls. "I'm not leaving my daughter out here with a wolf on the prowl, even if she is a stupid brat."

"She probably just went to a neighbor's house. Come back in and put the gun away and we'll make some calls."

"Put the gun away? This gun is the only thing standing between you and that wolf, woman! How dare you order me to do anything. You're not the boss around here, I am!" Three quick strides and he closes the distance between them.

"Of course, of course you're the boss, Clark, I just thought—"

Barb yelps as he strikes her. "And there's your whole problem. You should let me do the thinking. You ain't too bright, you know that."

Hannah pushes at me and groans pitifully, but I hold my ground.

"Yes, yes, of course Clark. I'm sorry," Barb says from below him. The hit must've knocked her off her feet.

Clark moves away from her and toward the forest again, calling for Hannah. He pumps the shotgun, and I hear the rasp of fingers grabbing fabric. He shouts, "Woman, why're you still here? Get back in the house!"

"Please Clark, please. Don't hurt my baby girl." Barb must be clutching at his clothes in desperation.

Clark shoves her away. "I told you I'm the boss here." And then his words are reduced to incoherent shouting as he strikes Barb again, and then again.

Hannah wails, pushing past me with panic-strong arms, and runs out of the hollow. "Stop! Mama!"

Clark stops hitting his wife. "Hannah? You stupid girl. Look what you made me do."

Barb gurgles wetly. Hannah runs to her, but ends up tussling with Clark. I can't see the fight, but I can hear it, grunts and whimpers, Hannah crying "No!"

She kicks him in the stomach; I know from the sudden *whuff* of air from his lungs. He wheezes, no doubt doubled-over with pain. Hannah scrambles across the slick ferns to her mother and lets out a long, low sob that raises every hair on my furry pelt.

I dash to her side, keeping close to the trees and ducking under ferns.

"I'm sorry, baby," Barb sighs. She gives a long, rattling, wheezing breath and grows quiet.

Hannah screams and screams. Clark staggers over to them. I hear the intake of breath as he draws back the gun.

Mustering every bit of strength in my old bones, I tackle him to the dirt. The gun flies from his hand and I hear it strike a tree nearby. All the air is knocked from his lungs when he hits the ground, and he gasps like a fish under me, flailing. He throws me off his chest and sends me spinning through the air.

I land hard, wriggling to my feet and scampering off into the brush before he can rise.

Hannah stands just as the rain starts again. I can hear her breathing hard and squelching through the mud toward her father. She doesn't help him to his feet, but rather casts about the ground looking for something.

The gun is easy for me to find, even in the rain. It smells wrong in the forest, a thing made of metal. I stand over it and let out a short, sharp howl that sounds almost like a dog's bark.

"Thank you, wolf," Hannah says, her hand brushing my ears as she bends to lift the weapon. I wonder whether she knows how to use it, but my question is answered when she hefts it to her shoulder and pumps it decisively.

Clark struggles to his feet, rasping. The cancer smell intensifies. "Hannah, bring me the shotgun," he gasps.

"You killed Mama," Hannah says through gritted teeth. "I'm gonna give you exactly what you deserve."

The gunshot is deafening. I can't see what's happening, and now I can't hear much either. When the ringing clears enough for me to hear again, the two of them are grunting, and there's the sound of feet squelching in mud and the slap of flesh hitting flesh.

"Give me the damn gun," Clark orders. "You don't know what you're doing with that thing."

"You bastard! You killed her!"

Thunder crackles and lightning zips across the sky. My vision is bright white for a split second, and I can see the hazy, gray silhouettes of a slender teenage girl and a huge man struggling over a shotgun. She lets go, and he staggers back to fall over in the mud.

Darkness closes over us again. I follow Hannah as she runs back to the house, keeping to the bushes that edge the yard. She opens the screen door and fumbles with the knob for the interior door. She makes a discouraged moan when the door doesn't open.

Clark staggers out of the trees. He laughs and I hear the jingle of house keys as he mocks his daughter. Of course he locked her out. He wouldn't want her sneaking back into the house while he's out here looking for her. He squelches up the lawn toward us. "Where's your dog friend now, eh?"

With a desperate, strangled warcry, Hannah rushes her father, driving them both to the ground. I bound after her and follow the stench of booze and cancer to land on Clark's chest. This time, I don't give him a chance to throw me off. I open my jaws and place them around his neck. I let him feel the sharp points of my teeth, let him know how much self-control I'm choosing to exercise. He freezes beneath me, going stiff with terror.

Hannah gains her feet and stands over us, breathing hard in the rain. I wait while she decides. She speaks softly, first, so I can't hear it under the drumming of my own heartbeat and Clark's, and then she shouts with a guttural growl: "Do it. DO IT."

Clark thrashes but it's too late. I bite down hard, latching onto his neck. Hot blood spurts into my mouth as I rip out his windpipe. Spitting out the chunk of flesh, I back away. He gurgles and flails. His death throes are over quickly.

The rain washes the vile taste of human blood from my mouth. I trot over to Hannah, who sobs and shivers. I press my head against her hand.

"What will I do now, wolf?" she whimpers, stroking my fur.

I lick her palm, and then look up at her. Lightning courses across the sky again and Hannah issues a little gasp. "You have the moon in your eyes."

Nuzzling her arm, I open my mouth and close it gently over her hand. I let her feel the sharp points of my teeth, as I did her father, but again, I wait while she decides. The last bite changed her life, and so will this one.

She stares off into the woods for a few long moments before turning back to me.

"Do it," she whispers.

Moments later, her hand bearing a few fresh puncture marks where my teeth pierced her flesh, we walk into the forest together. When the rain stops and I sense the moon peeking through the clouds, I throw my head back and howl. Hannah follows suit, her human voice becoming richer and darker until it's the voice of the wolf. Sheathed in fur, we make our way into the heart of the forest. My forest. Our forest.

# PUBLICATION HISTORY

"Tiny Teeth" originally published by *Pseudopod*, August 2019

"Rest in Peace" originally published in *Bless Your Mechanical Heart*, April 2014

"Madre" originally published in *The Arcanist*, March 2018

"Following Girls Home" originally published in *Something Good to Eat*, October 2020

"A Grace of Finer Form" originally published in *Novus Monstrum*, October 2023

"Chorus of Whispers' originally published in *Stitched Lips*, February 2021

"Dylan" originally published in *On Wings of Steam*, May 2022

"Take the Fire from Her" originally published in *Love Letters to Poe*, May 2021

"Nana" originally published in *Monsters in Spaaaace!* November 2019

"The Last Monster of the Nine Realms" originally published in *Origins!* June 2020

"A Legacy of Ghosts" originally published in *Never Too Old to Save the World*, February 2023

"The Moon in Her Eyes" originally published in *Burnt Fur,*
April 2020

# ABOUT THE AUTHOR

Sarah Hans is an award-winning writer, editor, artist, and teacher whose stories have appeared in more than 40 publications, including *Apex Magazine* and *Pseudopod*. Her most recent project is the cat-filled horror novella *Asylum*; she previously published the bug-filled horror novel *Entomophobia*, the demonic dark fantasy novella *An Ideal Vessel*, and her first short fiction collection, *Dead Girls Don't Love*. She lives in Ohio with her partner, an amazing kid, more pets than she can afford, and enough craft supplies to keep her busy for the next 200 years.

# ALSO BY SARAH HANS

### An Ideal Vessel

Not long ago, Zuzanna Uritski was a cleaner at the 1893 Chicago World's Fair, Archibald Campion was the Fair's most imaginative engineer, and Elspeth was a lifeless automaton. But now? Now they're demon hunters, pursuing an ancient evil that has traveled across universes to take residence in one of history's most famous serial killers. Travel to an alternate history where no one is safe from demon possession, automatons are self-aware, and the world's greatest hope lies with a clever engineer, a dauntless young woman, and a paladin from another world.

### Dead Girls Don't Love

Do you enjoy creepy stories about people who don't quite fit in? *Dead Girls Don't Love* is a collection of poignant tales for the outsider in all of us. For a domestic violence victim, there is no life after death--but could there be revenge? Can a woman returning to her life after 40 years with the fae remember how to be human?When two Buddhist monks travel to China to spread the dharma, will they survive the unspeakable horror they find instead?What really happened when the Big Bad Wolf ate the lonely grandmother living in the woods?Will the love between two zombified women help them break the spell that binds them in eternal servitude?And, perhaps most importantly, can an Elder God find true love?These and many more fascinating questions will be answered on the pages within, if you dare to read them. But be warned: the strange and horrifying realities contained in *Dead Girls Don't Love* may haunt you long after you close the back cover.

# DRAGON'S ROOST PRESS

**Dragon's Roost Press** is the fever dream brainchild of dark speculative fiction author Michael Cieslak. Since 2014, their goal has been to find the best speculative fiction authors and share their work with the public. For more information about Dragon's Roost Press and their publications, please visit:

http://www.thedragonsroost.biz